Letters From Johnny

ESSENTIAL PROSE SERIES 184

Canada Council **Conseil des Arts**
for the Arts **du Canada**

ONTARIO ARTS COUNCIL
CONSEIL DES ARTS DE L'ONTARIO

an Ontario government agency
un organisme du gouvernement de l'Ontario

Canadä

Guernica Editions Inc. acknowledges the support of the Canada
Council for the Arts and the Ontario Arts Council.
The Ontario Arts Council is an agency of the Government of Ontario.

We acknowledge the financial support of the Government of Canada

Letters From Johnny

WAYNE NG

**GUERNICA
EDITIONS**
TORONTO · CHICAGO · BUFFALO · LANCASTER (U.K.)
2021

Michael Mirolla, general editor
Julie Roorda, editor
David Moratto, cover and interior design
Avery Ng, cover illustrator
Guernica Editions Inc.
287 Templemead Drive, Hamilton, ON L8W 2W4
2250 Military Road, Tonawanda, N.Y. 14150-6000 U.S.A.
www.guernicaeditions.com

Distributors:
Independent Publishers Group (IPG)
600 North Pulaski Road, Chicago IL 60624
University of Toronto Press Distribution,
5201 Dufferin Street, Toronto (ON), Canada M3H 5T8
Gazelle Book Services, White Cross Mills
High Town, Lancaster LA1 4XS U.K.

First edition.
Printed in Canada.

Legal Deposit—First Quarter
Library of Congress Catalog Card Number: 2020945609
Library and Archives Canada Cataloguing in Publication
Title: Letters from Johnny / Wayne Ng.
Names: Ng, Wayne, author.
Series: Essential prose series ; 184.
Description: Series statement: Essential prose series ; 184
Identifiers: Canadiana (print) 20200327399 | Canadiana (ebook) 20200327402
| ISBN 9781771835770 (softcover) | ISBN 9781771835787 (EPUB)
| ISBN 9781771835794 (Kindle)
Classification: LCC PS8627.N318 L48 2021 | DDC C813/.6—dc23

For my grandfather, Ng Men Chem, who came to Canada by boat in 1911 from Hong Kong, and lived his last days with us in Toronto, on Henry Street.

PART ONE

LETTERS TO PENPAL

Dear Penpal

My name is Johnny Wong I am in grade 5 and go to Orde street public school and I live in Toronto. Mrs Clover is my teacher. She said I have to do a riting project like rite to a pen pal. She said a pen pal is like a best friend in a far away place. She said she will exchange these letters with a grade 5 class in Idaho every month. I am sorry but I have a for real friend now. His name is Rollie. He rents a room beside us except we have the biggest room in the house and we share the washroom and the kitchen with him and two ~~younivercidy~~ univercidy students in the rooms down stairs. Rollie is rich. He says he is in the ~~awqwasition~~ ocwasition of fine things and buys and sells and trades shiny things like forks and jewals and really old money. My mother likes that I have a friend who does not tease me. Rollie is very kind. Some times I want to call him dad but my for real father is in Vancoover. It was Rollie who gave me my first pack of hockey cards. Now I have 90 cards. Some day I hope to get a Dave Keon rookie card. So I do not need another friend. Unless you can make the new student Barry Arble stop calling me names and getting me into trouble.

Your friend,
Johnny Wong

Dear Penpal

I do not no what to rite. Mrs Clover said I could rite any thing. She said why not rite about ~~Cebbec Qebec~~ Kebec. But I know nothing about Kebec except that some body is all ways blowing up bombs there and wants to go away. So I picked riting about my faverit hockey team the Toronto Maple Leafs. My faverit player is Dave Keon. He won the award for fairest and hardest working player two times and one for being the best player in the play offs. What is your faverit team. Please do not say the Montreal Canadians. I asked Mrs Clover if Dave Keon could be my pen pal too but she said no because hockey players treat woman like ~~cattel catell caddle~~ cows. But I have never seen any cows at hockey games. Or woman neither. ~~Axsept~~ Except in the stands.

> *Your friend,*
> *Johnny Wong*

Dear Penpal

Mrs Clover said I have to rite enough letters to fill a yellow envelope before she sends them to you. She said I should rite about my home and family or our friends and what it is like in Canada or else I get another detenshin. We live near the univercity of Toronto beside queens park and near china town. Do you have a china town in Idaho. We are on Henry street where many chinese live. There are many gwhy low on the street too. gwhy low is what my mother calls white people but she never says that when Rollie is around. Many of them are rich and have houses all to them selfs. My biggest enemy Barry Arble moved into the house at the corner of Henry street and Baldwin street. He said he was in jewvee for beating up people but he was not afraid. He said if I dont smarten up he will get them to send me to jewvee too so I pushed him then Mrs Clover came over and made me stand by the wall even though it was his fault. That made me wonder if he could really get me sent to jewvee because it would be bad being away from mother plus how will father find me. The Catwoman next door to us is the scariest gwhy low. Rollie is my faverit gwhy low. He has a beerd and mustash and side burns. He says it is his Castro look. He is from Mane, United States. That is beside New found land. Is Mane near Idaho. My mother said he is a draft doger. But I have

5

never seen him run. He has lots of friends down the street. They play gitar drink beer and smoke until very late at night. One time Rollie thru his cigaret into Meany Mings garden. She got real mad and began to wave her skinny bean pole arms at Rollie. He worn his make love not war t shirt and pretended to be her by skwinting his eyes and swearing with fake chinese words. But I know he really likes chinese people because he said Mao was a groovy dude and a friend of people everywhere. That made me think that if the bombers from Kebec attack Canada China will come to our rescue. I told this to mother and she agreed.

Your friend,
Johnny Wong

Dear Penpal

Yesterday after dinner I went to Rollies room. He showed me his new ocwasition a color tv. He let me play with it while he read his book. I tried all the channels and stopped at the news that said 3000 sticks of dienomite was stolen in the last 2 months and that police expected the FLQ to target more ~~guvment~~ guverment buildings.

Rollie said them frenchies really know how to stick it to the man.

But the sticks were to blow up bildings and not a man I said.

He laffed and gave me a high five and said you kill me brother.

I asked him why people were blowing up bombs in Kebec.

He put his book down. He said people were mad at the man.

I looked at him and he could tell I did not understand.

Look he said the man could not be trusted because the man divides people and confuses them. It makes them questions themselves. Why you asking.

I did not really ask. But he kept talking.

He said confusing the masses puts money in the hands of the rich and some kind of military sportsplex.

He could tell I did not get it especially about the

man. I wanted to ask who is this man except I would look dum. So I did not.

He said its like this teenager Holden Call field in this book I love.

He showed me the book. It was called Catcher in the rye.

Rollie said Holdens really pissed off at the world and people. He always sees the worse in things and he doesnt even really know why. Its like hes just uncomfortable in his own skin and really needs to bust loose to find answers. That is what these french dudes are doing.

I asked if the FLQ were teenagers.

Rollie laffed again. He said they were probably not teenagers but that Canada is. Still I did not get it. Then he said that america had there own great war when they were about 100 years old. He said that is pretty young for a country. America had to go through some heavy stuff like a civil war. They had to figure out what they were about. Canada is 100 years old which he said was young and is going through the same kind of crap. That was his word and not mine.

Still I did not get it. He told me not to sweat it so I found Adam 12 on channel 2.

Your friend,
Johnny Wong

Dear Penpal

After school I went on a patrol of the nayberhood. I know all the streets and short cuts and alley ways and which fences to jump if I was under attacked. I know who likes to sit around doing nothing and who lives in what house. One time I found in the lane way between Henry street and McCaul street near Skinny farts house a empty garage that looks like it was ready to fall down. The ground is all dirt and paint cans and bottles of different colored lickwits are every where. I do not think any body has been inside in a long time but me. Nobody goes there so it is my favorite hiding spot except when it gets dark I go home but first to Rollie's room .

I told Rollie that I had to rite. He said far out man. Reading and riting is good. It is the key to stopping capitalising and 3rd world explorations. Then he gave me a dictionary. He said he will give me a nickel for every time I use it. He said he would trust me to keep a honest count. Man to Man. This time when he said man I knew what he was talking about. Then he gave mother another bottle of wine and more flowers. I am very happy that he is mothers friend too.

> *Your friend,*
> *Johnny Wong*

Dear Penpal

If you came to my street you could tell where most of the chinese live. They all grow vegetables. My mother grows red spinach peas and some times bitter ~~melins~~ melons too but I can not stand them. Do you like bitter melons. Meany Ming has the biggest garden. Her for real name is not really Meany Ming. Every body calls her that because she yells at people from her garden all the time with the same kitchen ~~aperin aprin~~ apron and over alls and thick glasses like a fish tank ready to fall down but do not and she watches every thing and every body mostly to make sure nothing comes near her vegetables. One time I saw her scare off a cat just by looking at it when it got near to her garden. Lots of times my ball fell over her Great Wall as Rollie calls it. She yelled at me and complained to my mother who also yelled at me. Still I never got my balls back. Some times I wish Meany Ming would just die.

Your friend,
Johnny Wong

Dear Penpal

Last night Meany Ming and the Catwoman got into a big fight. It is not the same Catwoman like in Batman. We just call her that because she has 6 cats. Mother says she must have 10 cats because it smells so bad in her back yard. On really hot days it smells like boiled pee. There are so many climbing in and out of her back window. Plus the Catwoman is really creepy. She lives beside us and Meany Ming is on the other side of her. Catwomans house is small and is always dark and looks like it is ready to fall down and she dresses like a rubbee. That means a really poor and dirty person but mostly dirty. One time Rollie and I were playing hockey and I shot a ball that almost hit one of her cats by accident. She got real mad. I could see her crooked yellow teeth and long finger nails. She said that if I did not smartin up someone will call childrens warfare because I was wild and for hanging around pot heads like Rollie.

Later I asked Rollie what a pot head was and he laughed and said they are the smart dudes with ~~unpolooted~~ un-polluted minds. But I was nervis. What if someone did take me away from mother. Father is already gone. I would have no body left. I hated her for saying that just after Barry Arble also said I had to smartin up or I could go to jewvee too. She is evil. Did I tell you I think she has long hair growing out of her ears and nose. So the fight started when Meany Ming said there was cat poo in her garden and she banged on the Catwomans door. I could hear them even with my favourite show Mannix on. It stars Mike Connors who plays a private ~~investigador~~ investigator who knows karate. His secretary is Gail and he has a police friend named Artie. Do you like Mannix. So I went outside to see. Meany Ming waved a shovel and screamed in chinese and a little bit of english. Meany Ming said your dirty cats pooed in my garden. But really she said a bad word. Then she said next time I will set out ~~poysin~~ poison. Then we see how much you like it. The Catwoman did not step out of her house but I could see her fist in Meanys face. I herd her yell if you touch any one of my cats I will kill you. Then she slammed the door. It was a great fight. I think Catwoman treats her cats like they was her children and that she would protect them to her death. Just like Meany Ming would for her vegetables.

Your friend,
Johnny Wong

Dear Penpal

When I got home from school yesterday the street was filled with police cars and a ~~ambulens~~ ambulance in front of Meany Mings house. The ambulance people carried a body covered up. But I could see muddy black boots and I thought this is my first for real dead body I ever seen. Have you ever seen a dead body too. Then I thought who else could it be but Meany Ming. Soon all the children and grown ups in the ~~nayberhood~~ neighbourhood came and they were very nice to me and asked me what happened. Because I did not know all I could say was that it was Meany Ming. Then Barry Arble came on his bike. He said I must have killed her with my ugly looks. All the children laughed. I wanted to smack him but my mother came running out of the house and dragged me inside. She said eye-yuh lots of trouble poor Mrs Ming. I asked her what happen but she just shaked her head and looked sad. I looked out the window. Barry was still talking to people like it was his side of the street but he lives down at Baldwin street so it is really my side. Then mother holded my hand so tight that it hurt. She made me promise to not get involved and stay away from police and to say nothing. I said yes mother. Then starting with our house and the univercity students downstairs the police went and talked to every body on the street. Rollie was not home yet.

Mother told them she herd nothing and saw nothing. The police asked if any body else herd any thing or knew if any body would want to hurt Meany Ming. I wanted to say Catwoman should be a suspect. But mother looked at me hard so I just stared at the floor and shaked my head but I also peeked at his gun and was going to ask to see the bullets too. But I did not. The police stayed on the street until it was dark. They put yellow police tape around the house. I was going to tell mother about the fight between Meany Ming and the Catwoman but she gave me some thing. It was a letter. She said it was from my useless father. When my mother says some body is useless it is the worst thing she can say about anybody. Then she said some swear words in chinese that I can not say to you. My mother and father used to fight. Then he went away to Vancoover. In the letter father said he was good and hoped to come home soon. He told me to study hard listen to mother always tell the truth and stay out of trouble. Mother did not let me go out that nite. This time I listened.

Your friend,
Johnny Wong

Dear Penpal

I feel bad for wishing Meany Ming was dead. Now I think I will stop wishing for Barry Arble to die too. Every body at school is talking about Meany Ming. Some people think there was a accident. Some people think all her enemies did the job. Mrs Clover thinks she may have died of natural causes and told us we were rude and disrespectful for talking like this and that she would give us detenshins after school if she heard another word. But I know what really happened.

> *Your friend,*
> *Johnny Wong*

Dear Penpal

Mother and I watched a very boring show called This Land. She likes to practice her english and see other parts of Canada. Then some special news came on. They were very serious. It was about a british diplowmat in Montreal named James Cross. He was kidnapped by delivery men disguised with a birthday present. I do not know what a diplowmat is but he must be important to get presents delivered. They surprised the maid with guns and charged in. The kidnappers said they want 23 prisoners freed or else they will kill James Cross. I thought 23 for one is not a fair trade unless it is for Dave Keon so no way will the police go for it. I asked mother why the maid did not carry a gun. She looked at me like it was a stupid question but then she said maybe she did but the delivery men were too fast.

> *Your friend,*
> *Johnny Wong*

Dear Penpal

Today mother was in a very good mood. She said every body in China town was talking about Canada and China being friends again even tho the United States and every body is against China and maybe some day she could bring her mother to live with us. She gave me 2 pork buns for a early dinner then we went to go to Kensington market to do laundry. She calls it the jewish people market but I do not see any body who looks jewish but if I did I would not know any way. They should call it the chicken and egg market because there are alive chickens plus ~~pijins pijons pegins~~ pigeons and rabbits in cages plus fish and big trays of eggs for sale and lots of vegetables and fruits in big piles. In Kensington every body speaks bad english and is new to Canada accept me because I am born here so that makes me some thing else. My favourite part here is to watch mother argue with the people before she pays. One time mother was going to make me her special fish jook and wanted a big bag of fish heads then she blamed the man for putting his finger on the scale. They got into a fight and the man squinted his eyes up and pretended to talk chinese then mother said some thing about his mother coming from a goat and a monkey but I am not sure because her english is so bad I can not get it. Then she threw the fish heads back at the man and they exploded all over him. The man started to swear in another language and waved his fist at mother who did the same back to him. Even though there was no kicking it was a great fight.

Then we went in to Sasmart. Mother made me try some Dash running shoes then let me go explore the store. There are many plates hanging on the walls with pictures of jesus with lots of people eating on a long table and many snow globes of jesus being born and ~~cookoo~~ cukoo clocks of the 3 wise men and lots of clothes and shoes. I tried on some cowboy boots and walked around. Mother saw me and laughed. She looked around and saw that the store owner and other customers were busy watching tv about the kidnapping in Kebec and that the police think it is the FLQ. Because no one was looking when mother tried on some cowboy boots too and added different kinds of hats. She pretended to shoot me and I pretended to die but knocked over a row of jesus on a cross. A woman came by and gave us a mean look. We said sorry and took our boots off and put the hats back. We left the store laughing and holding each other. Sometimes just because mother made father go away I forget that she is not mean all the time.

Your friend,
Johnny Wong

Dear Penpal

Mrs Clover reminded us that she will collect these letters next week. I hope you will write back. I hope you collect hockey cards or Spiderman comics. Who is your favorite villan. Mine is Doc Oc because he has four arms not counting his for real ones. Having a pen pal is not so bad after all. I am thinking about writing to Dave Keon at the same time. Now I write from home and school. I can tell you secrets and you will not laugh. Not like Rollie. Yesterday I went to his room. He was cleaning silver candle sticks. I told him I think maybe Meany Ming did not die by accident. I said I figured it out and have a suspect. He stopped cleaning and looked like I stole his hockey cards. I said Meany Ming was very mean to people. May be somebody wanted to get her back. Some body like Catwoman. He laughed and laughed and said may be I was right because Catwoman was tough and eats cat food and would not put up with any poo. He really said a swear word. Then Rollie said he is a man of his word and proved it by giving me $1.45 for using the dictionary 29 times. I let him read some of the letters to you. He looked at me for a long time and smiled.

Brother you have a uneek voice and you are a gifted riter. You rite letters like storys.

I did not think he was going to say that but it felt good.

He made me promise me to never give up writing. Then he said do not be afraid to take risks with it. Maybe you can write a book some day. He told me he was real proud then he messed up my hair and we laughed. Then he showed me a 5 dollar bill and said I could have earned even more easy money if I used the dictionary more.

That is when I made a wish. I wished he was my best friend forever.

I used some of the money to buy a pack of hockey cards and some Popeye cigarets. I smoked while I opened the cards and got a Paul Henderson in it.

That night the police said on tv that Meany Mings for real name was Pui Ching Ming. I did not know that and that she was the widow of a Hong Kong jeweler and that she was murdered and robbed. I could not sleep good because the one who killed her was right next door and her name is the Catwoman. I wanted to tell mother but she never believes me any way.

Your friend,
Johnny Wong

Dear Penpal

After school today I saw people go into Meany Mings house. They were empteeing it. One of them was her son Kwong. He was always nice to me and used to live there until he got married. He gave me a shoe box. It had all the balls all the kids ever lost in her garden. He said his mother was really a lot like mine. His mother was very sad and missed her husband a lot and gardened like crazy to forget how lonely she was. I went inside and started to cry because it made me think how much I missed my father. Plus it could have been my mother instead of Meany Ming they carried out.

> *Your friend,*
> *Johnny Wong*

Dear Penpal

Today was supposed to be a special day. It was the first hockey game of the year for Dave Keon and the Toronto Maple Leafs. They were versing the Vancouver Canucks. But a special news report came on. Another kidnapping happened. Mother came to watch. The men on tv looked very sad. The man kidnapped this time was named Peeair Laport. This time it was during when he was playing football with his ~~nefhew~~ nephew outside. The kidnappers let him write a letter to the premiere of Quebec. Peeair Laport said his two brothers are already dead and that he is the only one left to look after his big family and that his death would create grief. That sounded bad to me. They showed an old picture of his family. They looked very happy. He had a son Jean who is 11 like me. Jean is french for John so he almost has the same name as me. And now he does not have a father either. You could tell he looks like his father because he has the same ears. He also has a daughter who is older but she does not look like the son. Sometimes I wish I had a brother but I would take an older sister if I had to as long as she liked super heroes and not dolls. Do you have brothers or sisters Pen Pal. The tv said the father loved his family and took his son fishing and tot him how to drive a golf cart.

Eye yuhh my mother said. That is so sad. Then she lighted a cigaret.

I did not say anything but it made me feel sad because I know what it is like when a father is suddenly gone. Then the hockey game came back and we lost 5–3 to Vancouver so I was in a bad mood even more.

Your friend,
Johnny Wong

Dear Penpal

Today Mrs Clover said I had to serve another detension for not listening when she was talking about how strong prime minister True dough is. Sorry but I think he would not be hard to beat up if you were a man. Also I think she likes him. But I do not care about getting a detension because I can write more when no body is around. Meany Mings garden is a mess. Her vegetables are in knots or falling down waiting to be picked. I think that even tho I never liked Meany Ming Catwoman has to pay for what she did. I think there is evidence if I can find where she stashed the goods. That means hiding the things she robbed from Meany Ming which is something I saw a thief that Mannix caught trying to do. Then I will be a hero. Father and mother will be proud. And may be they will be back together again and father and Rollie can be friends and take me to watch Dave Keon.

Your friend,
Johnny Wong

Dear Penpal

After dinner mother said she had to go visit a friend. She said I could watch some tv but had to go to sleep right after. I guessed she was going to go play mah jong. I made a plan to see what was inside Catwomans window. But first I waited until Adam 12 was over. A short wood fence that was ready to fall down was what I had to climb to get into the Catwomans back yard. I had to be careful because I did not want to get cat poo on my new white Dash running shoes. There were bushes and tall weeds but it was not a garden with neat rows like Meany Mings was. I went to go to the open window but stopped. I could see eyes in the bushes. Then more eyes popped. Then more. I tried to rush back over the fence but I tripped. I could not get up. My ankle hurt so much I yelled out. Cats jumped out of the bushes. Then the back door opened and light got in my eye. Someone stepped out. A scary voice said whos there. I crawled on the ground to the fence but did not get far. The scary voice said again whos there. I looked back. It was the Catwoman. She walked funny with a cane in her hand. She got closer and closer. I thought she was going to beat me to death. I started to cry and begged that she not hurt me. She said my name. Then she asked what I was doing here. But her voice was not so scary this time. She looked at me and saw me holding my foot. She bended down and took off my shoe then my sock. She moved my foot a little and touched it in different places. I cried out. It is only a sprain she said. It is not broken like mine. Lucky you. Give me your hand. I looked at her but was too afraid to move. She looked at my house and said she would call my mother who will not be too pleased with me sneaking into peoples yards at night. I knew mother will kill me but I could not run away. I took her hand. She pulled me up to her door. You will not believe this but I went into the Catwomans house.

She put me on a sofa and made me put my leg on a chair. She dragged her foot to get ice. I could smell no cat poo or pee any where. I was very surprised that it was very clean and tidy with more books than any where except the library. There were pictures of a happy young woman dressed like a nurse in the army who looked like her. She came back with a bag of ice for my foot. But she was moving funny. When she sat down her face twisted up. She looked at my foot. But she never looked at me. We did not say any thing. I moved my leg and the bag of ice dropped. That made her almost jump out of her chair. It was like she was more afraid than me even in her own house. Then one long haired cat came and rubbed against my leg. She said that is Sidney a ~~Manecoon~~ Mane coon. It purred against me. It had long whiskers. She said Sidney is charming but also a rascal and do not trust him. What is a Mane coon I asked. They come up from the US and are good hunters she said. I told her Mane is where Rollie is from. He is charming too. But I can trust him. How many cats do you have I asked. She almost smiled. 8 cats she said. But they always bring friends over. I asked her why you have so many cats. She said cats have ~~personalady~~ personality and really they are easy to look after. They dont need much. Unlike humans who need to belong. Most of my cats except for Sidney are very loyal and would never hurt any body for no good reason. So remember to stay away from cats from Mane. She said does the ankle feel better. It did. Keep off your ankle when you get home she told me. I looked at her cast and asked what happened. She said she broke her ankle 2 weeks ago avoiding stepping on Sidney. I asked her if I could write on her cast. She said maybe later. I was going to write Catwoman Lives. When I got home mother was not there. I heard her come upstairs and was going to tell her that I did not think Catwoman was the killer but my ankle hurt and I knew she would yell at me for sneaking out and getting hurt. So I just pretended to sleep until I fell asleep for real.

Your friend,
Johnny Wong

Dear Penpal

You will not believe what I found after school. In the lane way there was a big orange bean bag with a hole in it. I think someone left it there for garbage. I jumped on it and lots of white bits of plastic came out. I dragged it to the garage and it made a trail like it was a popcorn machine. Now I have something to sit on when I am thinking about the murder. If Catwoman is not Meany Mings killer who was. I knew she had many enemys because she was so mean. I thought of who went near her house. The mail man always does. He is a nice and friendly man that I do not want to suspect him. Then one time I was outside bouncing a ball I seen a short gwhy low lady with a suit case going to all the houses selling avon make up. When she came to our house mother told her to go away. Then she went to Meany Mings house and was let in. The avon lady was inside for a long time before she came out. Then Meany Ming came out to pick some melons. I could hear her humming a song and when she turned to me she had bright red cheeks and lips and was in a good mood. That made me wish mother had let the avon lady in. Then I thought maybe while the avon lady was inside she cased out Meanys place and came back to do the job. Yesterday I saw on Adam 12 that it is mostly family and people who you know and live around you that will kill you. That makes Meanys son Kwong a suspect. It made sense because he probaly had a key and knew where her jewwels were. But it also means mother and Rollie and me are suspects but that is stupid. So it has to be the mail man, the avon woman or Kwong. I wanted to ask Rollie what he thought so I left the garage.

It was almost dinner time so I went straight to the kitchen and could smell mothers yummy toefu and spicy pork dish cooking but she was not there. I could hear music coming from Rollies room. I went upstairs. The music was Rollies favorite beetles song Let it Be. I wanted to tell him about the other suspects and ask if he ever had a Mane coon cat and tell him Catwoman could not have killed Meany Ming because Catwoman had a broken ankle already and I did not think she was a killer even though we all thought she was creepy. I went to his room and heard him laugh. Then I heard mother laugh. My stomach started to feel funny. I opened the door to peek. Mother and Rollie were dancing.

I could hear mother say no more time to dance. Johnny coming home any minute now.

Rollie reached into his back pocket and pulled something that shined and handed it to mother. He said it was a present for her.

Mother looked at it with a big smile like it was a surprise. She holded it like it was a first edition rookie card of Dave Keon. Soo beautiful Rollie where you get that.

It was a unexpected bonus he said.

Then she got scared. Eye yuh that is Mrs Mings dragon pendant. She gave it back to Rollie and stepped away.

Rollie said relax we could go away and take Johnny too.

Go away I thought. I do not want to go any where in case father comes home.

Mother asked if Mrs Ming was dead because of him.

He shaked his head and said no no its not like that. The old lady surprised me in the dark. I did not mean to do it but it was too late. I tried to help but she was dead before I could do any thing.

Then mother shaked her head and pushed him away. You are a murderer.

I could not move and felt stuck for a long time even though it was not long. But before Rollie or mother said anything else I ran down the stairs as fast as I could. I went up Henry street on to College street and just kept going even though my ankle still hurt from falling in Catwomans yard yesterday. Then around Yonge street a police man stopped me. The police man looked like the GI Joe adventure team man with sun glasses I always wanted. He looked around at every thing like we were going to be attacked. It was a mean look. I do not know how he could see any thing in the dark with the sun glasses on.

He asked if I was a run away. When he talked his mouth hardly moved.

I wanted to tell him that Catwoman is not what she looks like and can not be a suspect any more. I wanted to say that some friends can be charming with personality. I wanted to tell him that Rollie is from Mane like Sidney. And that Rollie could trick people like mother and could hurt someone. And he did and that someone was Meany

Ming. Then I remembered what mother said. To not get involved. And what father said. Stay out of trouble. So I told the police man I got lost and that I live at 56 Henry street. Beside the Catwoman. When the police man brought me home mother thought I was in trouble and was ready to yell at me. Rollies eyes were all red but he looked like he saw a ghost and turned away but the police asked him for his name and where he lived. Rollie said Roland Brown and that his room was next door.

The police man looked at Rollies Che Guevara tee shirt then he wrote something down then asked if Rollie had an American accent.

Rollie said no but sometimes he talks that way because he lived near the US border.

Where the police man asked.

In New Brunswick near Mane.

I think Rollie lied.

The police man asked to see Rollies id.

Rollie said hey man I know my rights. You cant just question me unless you have cause and I know you got nothing. This conversation is over.

The GI Joe police man stepped towards Rollie then stopped. Okay Mr Roland Brown I'll be seeing you he said.

I thought for sure there was going to be a fight in our house but this time it would be for real and scary.

Instead the police man left. Mother yelled and yelled at me and then at Rollie. Rollie looked at me like I turned everybody against him. I said nothing to mother or Rollie. I did not care and ran straight to write to you.

Dear Penpal. I do not know what to do. I want to run away but have no where to go. I hope you get this soon and write back.

Your friend,
Johnny Wong

Dear Penpal

I ran into class and gave Mrs Clover the letters. She said she was going to send them Monday. That was 5 days away. I said why not now. She said she had to review some of them. She did not tell us that before or maybe she did and I did not listen. I went to take mine back but she stopped me and told me to sit down. I watched her put every bodys letters in separate big yellow envelopes and make a pile. I waited for her to leave the room but she did not. Then we had gym. I asked to go to the washroom and sneaked upstairs to our classroom and saw the pile of yellow envelopes and was about to take them all but Mr Ingles caught me and said no wandering and I should be in gym so he walked me back.

I went home for lunch but could not stop thinking if she was going to read my letters to you. Then after lunch she called me to her desk and said we were going for a walk. She said I live in a interesting neighbourhood with interesting people but that she did not know my father was in Vancouver. Then I got it. She read my letters. She walked me to principal Ingles. They talked with me about what I wrote. They kept asking if I was sure about what I saw and heard about Rollie and the jewel. I kept saying no. Then Mr Ingles said if I do not tell the truth the police will be called. I remembered what mother said. But I got scared. So I told the truth and he called the police any way. I hate Mr Ingles even more now that he is a big fat liar.

Two men with police badges came. They read my letters that were supposed to go to you. They are supposed to be private with secrets. Then they talked to me. The police man who looked the most handsome with neet side burns was very nice to me and kept saying what a good writer I was and good looking too. He asked if I knew kung fu and pretended to do moves on me. It was not funny. I wished that even though he was a police office I could chop him in the head then do a round house kick on the other police officer and then escape. The 2nd one never smiled and got close to me. He did not shave. His breath smelled like cheesies and ~~cigarets~~ cigarettes even from far away. He said it was against the law to lie to a police officer. You could go to jewvee you might not see your mother for a long time. I think that is what Rollie would have called blowing smoke. I think they were playing good cop bad cop but I also believed what he was saying. A murder happened and mother was involved. This was bad.

Mother came. I never seen her look so scared. The bad ugly cop talked to her like she was stupid. Then they really scared her. They said she knew that Rollie was a murderer and she did not tell the police. They said she could go to jail for ~~conspearacy~~ conspiracy and being a accomplished and whatever else they could think of.

Mother said, Rollie bad. Bad man. He tell lie. Not me. I know nothing. I do nothing wrong. She started to cry. I could not look.

They asked if we knew where Rollie was because he was not in his room and it looked like he packed up in a hurry. I was not sad that my only friend was gone. Instead I was mad. Very mad. He almost made me tell on the wrong person. And I am sure he made my mother like him even though she misses father. Mother stopped crying but I could tell how scared she was still. Then some lady took me into a room by myself and kept asking me dum questions like what mother feeds me. She did not even know that jook is rice porridge. I was tired. A long time passed. I got hungry. There were no donuts.

Then the two police man took us home. They warned us that they will find Rollie and that if we ~~asosheate ass-holesheate~~ associate with him we would be arrested. Mother said nothing to me. She is still saying nothing to me.

Your friend,
Johnny Wong

PART TWO

LETTERS TO MR. KEON

Dear Mr Keon

My name is Johnny Wong. I go to Orde Street public school. I am in Mrs Clovers class. She and Mr Ingles are sneaky. So is Rollie who used to be my best friend who is a murderer but I am not.

As the Captain of the Toronto Maple Leafs you are the only person I can trust. You always play fair and do your best. I want to keep writing. Maybe I will write a book some day like Rollie said. He is a murderer but he said I was good at writing and he gave me a dictionary and that is the only good thing about him and is not a lie. So I want to keep writing but this time not to the penpal so I came up with a plan for writing that will not get me into trouble this time. From now on I will write in secret to you. I will hide the letters in the basement under a box of my fathers clothes. My father is gone but when he comes back and takes me to Maple Leaf Gardens I will give you all my letters and you can show me how to make a book.

Thank you

> *Your Friend,*
> *Johnny Wong*
> *Orde Street Public School, Toronto*

p.s. I really like the rookie Darryl Sittler. I hope he will fit in too. Also who is your favourite super hero?

Dear Mr Keon

Who was your best friend when you were in grade 5? I bet he played hockey with you and did not steal and kill people like Rollie. After he disappeared and mother and me got grilled by the police we had to talk to someone from child warfare about our family. Mother cleaned the house and mopped the floor and made me put away my Batman utility belt and hockey cards that Rollie gave me. I could tell mother was scared but she hided it. When someone knocked I opened the door.

A woman said oh you must be Johnny they did not tell me you were such a handsome young man. Her eyes were blue like the Specific ocean and her hair was like goldielocks and covered the top of her long coat which looked like it was a Batwoman cape that covered her whole body.

Is your mother home Johnny?

Mother yelled in chinese, Johnny is that her?

I do not remember what I said but I let her in. She said her name was Barbra Twomanski.

She walked in with shoes that looked like leperds with big heels and made marks on mothers clean floor. I knew this made mother go from scared to mad. Mother shaked her hand but never stopped staring at her. Barbra

Twomanski started to take her cape off. She asked something but I just looked at her dress that was shorter than her cape. It was all black except the sleeves and collar were leopard spots with a zipper that went reall far down.

Johnny she asked. Johnny? Where can I leave my coat?

I took her cape but did not know what to do. Finally mother took it and hanged it up. The lady brushed something off her dress and said she was sorry that the translator was sick and asked if I could help her out. That means I had to explain everything in chinese to mother.

You have a groovy home. The woman said her job was to make sure I was looked after and safe. She giggled like a girl and said she was sorry because she was kind of new at this job and wanted to do a good job.

Mr Keon this is one of my biggest secrets ever and you cannot tell any body. But Barbra Twomanski is very pretty like Shirley Jones in the Partridge Family but not so old. Maybe you could meet her and see for yourself.

Mother elbowed me and asked what she said so I told her. Then mother took a breath and smiled slowly at Barbra. This reminded me of the movies. Sometimes when I am good mother takes me to the double feature movies at the pagoda theatre. The last time there was a mother who was a farmer and a kung fu master. She was surrounded by band its. The farmer wiggled her toes and smiled at them just the way mother was doing right now. Then the farmer kung fu master did a round house kick and took the head off the band it leader and scared everybody away.

I was getting nervous because I could imagine mother doing it too. I looked at mothers toes and prayed they did not move. They did not.

Instead mother asked the woman in chinese if she was blind. Can you not see my son eats. Mother pinched my cheeks. Can you not see my son has a home. Why don't you mind your own bisnis.

I looked at mother then at Barbra Twomanski. I told Barbra that my mother said I eat so much that every day she has to go to china town to buy food. And she makes good wonton but I wanted to try beefarowknee. Then the woman said she always wanted to try real chinese food not the fake stuff like sweet and sour bo bo balls. Maybe we could have lunch together sometime she said.

I think I said yes but do not remember.

She said she was sorry but had to look around our house and went into the kitchen downstairs and looked into our part of the cup boards and refrigerator. She said we have lots of strange looking vegetables but no milk no cheese no bread.

I did not say that milk makes my tummy hurt and that cheese is too much money for mother. But I did tell a small lie and said mother and I finished all the bread with the pigeons in the park.

That's charming Johnny. She went back to our room and to the other side of the curtain where the bed was. Only one bed she asked. I nodded and said my mother usually sleeps on the couch so I get the bed except when I can not sleep and she comes to sleep with me. That made me feel embarrassed like I was a baby.

Mother gave me a mean look like she was a assassin and wanted me to get out of her way so she could just kill Barbra now.

Then Barbra went back to the kitchen for another look and saw the cup board above the refrigerator. Because she was tall it was easy to see in the cupboard and when I heard some bottles I knew she found mothers other Johnny. The one with the black boots and red jacket on a red label.

Barbra looked at mother who crossed her arms and looked away and said not mine.

She asked what time mother comes home and who are her friends.

I said I did not know exactly when because she comes home to have lunch with me and is already home from work making clothes before I get back and that mother has no friends who come over since Rollie disappeared. This is the truth. I did not tell her that on many nights mother leaves after dinner to wash dishes at Hung Fatt restaurant or sometimes plays mah jong with other woman down the street and sometimes comes home happy and one time she even gave me money without having to do anything. That is when I go out on my patrols in the neighborhood with the garage as my base. Then she asked if I would ever lie to her. She looked so sad when she said it. This is very important she said. Nothing is more important to me than your safety. If your mother has any contact with that criminal she will be in big trouble. She said big 2 times. Not only that I'm worried she wont be able to keep you safe here. If you or she sees Mr Berry you are to notify the police immediately. I think you know him as Rollie.

Mr Keon what do you do when you get nervous. Like what if the goon John Ferguson of the Montreal Canadians verses you to a fight. Sometimes I get very quiet when I am nervous and I did that time when she said mother won't be able to keep me safe here. Was she saying I could go to jewvee.

Finally I said I understand.

Good she said and then she smiled again.

What she say mother interrupted.

They stared at each other with smiles like they were imagining each other about to die in a battle ready to happen.

Instead Barbra Twomanski said she thought it was enough for now.

I do not think she believed me. She said she has to continue to make sure we were both okay and would check on us again and will talk to mothers work and the school.

My mother said thank you for coming with a big fake smile.

After Barbra left mother starting yelling. Mostly when mother yells I think of other things and do not listen but this time I listened to everything she said. She said do not say anything to her. If I cannot keep my mouth shut and she loses her job we will not have money for food or a place to live and this was all my fault and if somebody takes me away it will be because I did not mind my own bisnis. Then she went downstairs poured Johnny in to a tea cup and made me go to my room without dinner witch is really bad like Pete Malloy in Adam 12 telling his partner Jim Read that he did not want them to be partners any more. I wanted to know if she was for real that I might get sent away. But if I did would I have to go live with Barbra and for how long. And if that happened how would father find me.

Your friend,
Johnny Wong

Dear Mr Keon

Yesterday after school mother said she was going to work late so after dinner I walked on College street past the police station. I kept going and went past Queens park past Bay street past Yonge street to Maple Leaf Gardens. I thought you might be back from beating St Louis 7-3 so I waited to see if you would come out from practice. When I got bored of waiting I walked around the building to look in the garbage bin in case anybody on the team threw out broken hockey sticks. Then I went to Eatons. I liked going all the way up and down the escalator. There was a crowd of people around the tvs so I investigated. Everybody was quiet then someone said bloody FLQ. The tv showed lots and lots of people cheering in french. Somebody cut up the Canada flag. The man on tv said poplar support for them was rising and that their goal was to separate from Canada.

A man beside the tv with a long rubbee coat made me think of detective Columbo said that they are going to win because they have more boys ready to shoot members of parliament than there are policemen.

Then we saw soldiers marching and guarding in Montreal. Then a man beside me who looked like Kernel Klink said it won't be long before they are stationed in Ottawa and probably Toronto.

Someone else said the frogs wont dare to revolt with the army out.

Then the tv showed a skinny man with glasses like Meany Mings argue that the government was using a sledgehammer to crack a peanut because this was not a state intersection. .

I wanted to see if there would be tanks and aircraft carriers but then Kernel Klink asked wear my mother was.

I looked at him and pretended that I did not understand then bowed and walked away. I went up to my favorite floor on the top. It had all the sofas and beds. I like the chairs that have wide arms and spin around like Captain Kirks chair. I started to get tired and went into the sofa section for a rest. I fell asleep and had a dream about the FLQ taking over Canada and father sending me on a special mission to rescue hostages from them. Then I dreamed that some bad men controlled the FLQ which means Frogs Living in Quebec and sended in thousands of frogs who brought me to there leader. The leader of the frogs said wake up kid wears your mother wake up.

Then I did wake up and a man with a french voice asked me wear mother was.

I was going to answer then thought if I tell them mother is working then Barbra will find out and someone will make me talk and someone will take me away. I had to buy some time so I told him in chinese how to boil noodles.

The man said a bad word and said he was going to make a call. I wanted to run but some one else came to watch me and he gave me a whole bar of Kit Kat. He raised his voice like I could not hear and said it is no egg roll or chop suey but its good eh. I think he was trying to be nice and funny but it was not.

I ate the Kit Kat really fast because I was hungry and it was so good.

Soon a woman police officer came. She was the tallest woman I ever saw in person even taller than the warfare woman Barbra. She bended down to me and smiled. She asked where was my mother. I said home but I did not really know. She asked if I knew where she could drop me off. I said 54 Henry Street.

Then the man with the french voice came back and said but you must call da child welfare, da CAS no? This child has been asleep for 40 minutes. He started drooling on one of the new velvet sofas. Maybe he peed in it too. This is unacceptable. He is abandoned or a run away. He must be put in a proper home.

I did not pee in my pants but after he said that I wish I did all over his velvet sofa. Plus I did not know what CAS was but thought of Barbra and what he meant by proper home but I guessed it did not mean with mother. I wanted to cry but holded it in and the police woman saw.

She said no sane mother would on purpose leave there son in a department store alone. Hes a wanderer. The woman police officer stood up and moved her hat. She looked down at the man and said this boy is well fed properly clothed has no apparent injuries and is not in any distress. I'll bet he has a mother who loves him. Come a long son. She gave me her hand. I smiled and grabbed it. I got to ride in a police car for the second time but this time with a police woman. She talked to me like a friend like she cared. She told me her family came over in a boat from ~~Eyeareland~~ Ireland. I wanted to ask if there were frogs there and if they ever had a revolution. But I did not. When the police car turned onto Henry street I saw Barry Arble riding his bicycle right near us. My mother ran out of the house towards the police car. Barry stopped and watched the police woman and me walk to my house. The police woman told mother everything was okay and not to worry. Then she asked about Mr Wong.

No mister Wong. Only me mother said.

I wanted to chop Barry in the head and charge him because he was listening and was going to spread lies again and tell everybody that I was caught stealing and murdering again. But then I remembered that you got the sportsman award for playing fair and not fighting. So I did not either. What should I do instead Mr Keon?

> *Your friend,*
> *Johnny Wong*

p.s. That night I woke up from a dream and heard someone in Catwomans yard. She came out to call her cats in and the light from her house showed someone who jumped over her fence and ran into the lane way. I thought it was Rollie except there was no moustache and I am not sure if it was a dream or for real.

Dear Mr Keon

Today at recess I pushed Patty Beeso into a puddle of water. I know I promised I would be like you Mr Keon and not fight and that hitting a girl is wrong but I was going for Barry Arble because he called me a stupid thief and murderer. I tried to tell him that it was Rollie who double crossed me and is the real thief and the real murderer plus a lier. He would not listen and the other kids started to chant good grief Johnnys a thief so I chased him around the yard and accidently pushed Patty Beeso.

I wanted to wish Barry Arble would die then I remembered Meany Ming died after I wished her dead so I was not sure any more. Then the lunch monitor came and took me to that big fat lier principal Ingles who was smoking and listening to the radio about the FLQ strangling a hostage to death and then stuffing him in a car near the airport in Montreal yesterday.

He pressed his cigarette into a tray and said what the hell do they want. Dam frog bastards I hope they catch them and hang them by there nuts. I started to giggle then the lunch monitor cleared her throat and told him about me kicking Patty Beeso. I thought he was going to yell and take out the ruler but instead he turned the radio down and put on a smile that never moved then told me to sit down. Then he sat beside me and put his hands on his knees. One of them shaked up and down like a jack hammer.

He asked me how I was.

It was really weird because I know he hates me. I thought it was a trap so I just said OK. I could see some gum stuck on his shoe. He asked me about mother and her friends. I said mother was fine.

He said he knew that the police are still looking for that no good commie draft doging murdering thief.

I wanted to say yes. Yes. It is him Rollie and not me who is the thief and a murderer. Please tell everybody in the school. Instead I said nothing because I guessed he wanted a reward for catching Rollie and thought maybe I knew where he was. So I did not say anything.

He put a hand on my shoulder and said I could talk to him about any thing. It was like he was playing a good cop except he was also a bad cop.

So I asked him what the FLQ was.

His smile went away. He said those are frog ~~basterd~~ bastard terrorists and then he got all red and said they were trying to separate from the country and stick it to the english but the army was going to kick there asses. Sorry Mr Keon for the bad words but that is what he said not me. I think he saw that he used bad words and stopped himself. I did not understand everything else but I did not like it. I think he was making fun of people from Quebec and that includes you.

He lighted another cigarette and sucked it hard then blew it out. He said to forget what I just heard and that all I needed to know was that our commie prime minister

Trudeau thinks he's a gun slinger and that he said just watch me. Then Mr Ingles raised his voice and said well I'm watching. The whole god dam country is watching. Calling in the army was ~~brellant~~ brilliant. I'll give him that. He might get this right after all. Then he gave me some gum. It was mint and not dubble bubble but I took it because I did not want him to get any redder. I saw his fingers were wrinkled like poor Meany Mings accept his fingers smelled like a ash tray. He said he was glad we talked and that he would not call mother this time. Then I thought for sure it was a trap.

That was good because mother is very nervous since Rollie disappeared. Then the principal made me sit in until recess was over which it was almost any way. On the way back to class I went to the washroom to see if any body was in there then took the long way back before returning to class.

Mrs Clover was talking about the news and she also said prime minister Trudeau would fix the problem in Quebec and asked if any body heard about what was going on there. I raised my hand. She said it was nice of me to join the class. I raised my hand higher. Then she looked away like it was now me setting a trap because I never raise my hand but this time I was really listening and knew the answer. She pretended to not see me but nobody else raised a hand and I could not hold it in so I said frog bastards kidnapped some body then he got stuffed in a car. Everybody laughed except her.

She said murder is not funny and she should send me to the office for that language but I talked back and said the principal said it first and also thinks the commie will fix it. Then I wanted to ask her what a commie was. But I did not.

Then she said well you seem to know lots about murder.

But I think she was saying about what happened to Meany Ming like it was my fault and not about this murder in Montreal.

This made everybody laugh again but this time I got really mad so for the rest of the day I pretended like she was invisible. Were your teachers mean to you too Mr Keon?

Your friend,
Johnny Wong

Dear Mr Keon

Ever since the kidnappings mother watches news all the time. And ever since the army was called she started to buy lots of extra food. She said it reminded her of when the Japanese came and they had to get lots of food and hide it. I could not sleep and got out of bed to watch the news with mother. There was a big funeral in a big church for the hostage Pierre Laporte who was strangled and stuffed in a car. His coffin was wrapped in a white and blue flag. The prime minister and premier of Quebec were there and lots of other people and police and soldiers. I do not know if you saw it on tv Mr Keon but everybody looked very sad. His family held hands. Pierre Laportes wife was all in black and looked very sad. My mother was also sad. She did not even send me back to bed. Instead she said it was very lucky Jean was not at home when his father was kidnapped and was out playing doge ball Doge ball is my favorite fis ed sport. His father was playing football with his nephew when the kidnappers came. The nephew would be Jeans cousin. I'll bet Jean wishes he was home when the kidnappers came so he could have saved his father.

Mother held my arm very tight. She said she could not afford to lose me. That I was everything to her.

She made me promise to stay away from mail boxes

and government buildings because the FLQ put bombs there. It was weird because mother never talked like that. I have to do everything to protect you she said. I did not know what she was talking about but it made me think that Jean also only has a mother left like me . If you dont count his sister. Do you have any brothers or sisters Mr Keon. How about a father? I bet he played with you all the time and teached you things and collected hockey cards.

This made me think about the last time I saw my father. He was not kidnapped. It was a long time ago but I remember it. I even remember the time he got me a ~~etchasketch~~ etch a sketch for Christmas. I was 4 years old. The last time I saw him he was fighting with mother. I used to just sleep thru them fighting but this was a big one and I pretended to sleep. She yelled at father and said he was a lier and could not ever trust him again. And that was the last time I seen or heard him. He left me a letter and said I will always be his son no matter what. Please do not tell any body this.

Your friend,
Johnny Wong

Dear Mr Keon

Everybody says there are bad men in Quebec and that the french are winers. But you are from there so I know they are wrong. Plus why are frogs revolting in Quebec? Is it because of the ddt? Mrs Clover said ddt is very bad especially for small animals. I guess like frogs.

> *Your friend,*
> *Johnny Wong*

Dear Mr Keon

Did you have a Woolworths in Quebec? One time Rollie took me there and we went crazy on the spinning stools and ate french fries. Yesterday I was in Woolworths looking for a Batman mask to go with my Batman shirt for Halloween when someone with a John Lenin mask and jean jacket came up to me. I know who John Lenin is because Rollie said he was the best beetles and that Paul was a sissy. Who is your favourite Mr Keon?

Hey brother, what's happening?

I knew the voice.

John Lenin raised his mask. I did not recognize him at first then he smiled. It was Rollie except his Castro hair was gone.

Your looking good. I miss my chinese connection Rollie said.

I stepped back because I was scared and did not know what to do.

Yo be cool, he said. I've always had your back, ain't that right?

I nodded.

Didn't I give you your first hockey cards, a viewmaster, your first dictionary?

I nodded hard this time. They were some of my best things.

Then he asked if he let me hang with him when no-body else would?

I nodded again but could not look up.

Didn't I protect you when that jive talking Meany Ming chased you with a rake?

Then you killed her I said to myself.

It was almost like he could read my mind because he said things did not happen the way the newspapers said. She was supposed to be asleep but she snuck up on him and swung without seeing her. He said how was he supposed to know her head would hit the radiator. It was a accident. It wasn't his fault. At least it's not what he wanted.

I looked away and asked him what did he want?

A police man walked by. Rollie put his mask back on then pulled me beside some shelves with fake moustaches and beards. He lifted his mask again. I just want to go home. I need to see my family. Back to Maine, to some backwoods cabin and wait out the man's war. That's what I should have done in the first place.

I did not know what to say. I believed he was lying again.

I need your help Johnny.

This time I looked right at him. What can I do, I'm just a boy.

I left some stuff in your apartment.

What?

A small box.

Then what do you need me for just go get it yourself.

What are you crazy man. The fuzz is everywhere. I'm not stupid, I saw the unmarked cars parked by the house.

So maybe they already found it I said.

He said he did not think so because fuzz aren't that smart and he did a good job of hiding it.

I did not understand and he saw that.

It doesn't matter Johnny. If they had already found it then your mother would be in jail.

I froze. I told him I did not understand.

Just listen up Johnny. Between the legs of the radiator by the window is a loose floor board. Its in tight so you'll need a hammer to drive in a screw driver between the boards. Like this. He looked around then pulled out a small nap sack with a tiny hammer and a long screw driver. He showed me what to do with it.

He said once I get the board out I'll find a small box. It will get him home across the border and he can lay low until the stupid war in Nam is over. That's all he needed.

Rollie always looks like he is having fun. He always smiles and laughs. But that time he looked very tired and wild like a rubbee. I wanted to be nice and say ok then I thought of the police and Barbra Twomanski and the principal and all the people who would be mad and would punish me by sending me to jewvee and away from mother.

I shaked my head and started to cry. I can't I said. I can't do it. I'll get in trouble.

He pushed me into a rack of costumes. You're going to do this. You know why?

I shaked my head.

He said Johnny if I get busted your mother gets in trouble.

So ask her to help.

Rollie laughed a little. Your old ladys a blast but she's panicky. I can't trust her like I can trust you. She'll get herself busted.

No I can't do it.

You have to. I don't want to do this Johnny but if I don't make it home I'll say she is part of everything. He said he would tell the police that mother was the mastermind. That mother cased out Meany Ming's place and besides her fingerprints were all over some hot items. Fingerprints don't lie he said.

So he was ready to rat out mother. I shaked my head and started to cry. Not true not true I said.

He slapped me in the face. It did not hurt but nobody except mother ever hit me.

Knock it off. Stop crying he almost yelled. He pulled a Scooby Doo mask over my face but it was too big and it was hard to breath and the plastic was scratchy.

He said he paid our rent for months while mother lost at mah jong down the street and he paid for the other Johnny on top of the refrigerator. She never asked questions he said, but she's not stupid. And you're not either.

Not true not true is all I could say.

Maybe. But if the fuzz believe just 1 per cent of it your mother does time. You know what I mean by that? Jail he said and I would wind up living with some jesus freak honkys out to save the world. First no dad now no mom. I will have nothing. Think about it, he said.

I did think about it and wanted to cry more but kept it inside this time.

He looked around then lifted the mask and let go of me. Sorry Johnny he said. Its been a rough few weeks for me. Do me this big favor and we all get on with our lives. I promise. No I swear.

I looked around then nodded. Okay I said.

Now there's a brother.

He made me repeat all the instructions until I got it right. It took me a few times because I was nervous.

Good. When you get it leave it behind the paint cans in that garage you hang at. I'll know. He put the hammer and screw driver in a paper bag and told me to wrap my coat around it.

I got to split he said. There's loads of heat around.

Then he went back to the street and was gone.

I did not know how he knew about my secret hang out. But that means he was following me and watching me. And maybe that really was him I saw in Catwoman's yard the other night. So he knows where I am and what I am doing.

Before he went he handed me a pack of hockey cards like nothing had happened and Meany Ming was still alive and he was still my best friend and I did not have you to write to. But it is not like that any more.

I went home and mother was watching the news. I looked at the radiator but could not see the floor boards edges clearly because it was dark. Then I heard the news that police continue to look for the killer of Pui Ching Ming. They said the suspect is Roland Berry but he also has an alias of Roland Brown. They said he is part of a gang who were breaking and entering Rosedale homes for sometime. They did not know who the other gang members are yet but police should be notified immediately if you see him as he should not be approached because he is dangerous.

Roland Berry and his gang. What if he does say mother is part of his gang. What if he says I am because I have his hammer and screw driver.

Mother looked at me. She said do not be scared. Rollie is long gone. He is too smart to come back.

But what if he does I asked.

He has no reason to come back. If he is that stupid just stay away. Mother will get in trouble. We will get in trouble. Let the police catch him. You understand me?

If the police do catch him can we still get in trouble I asked.

Why? We have done nothing wrong.

She saw that I was not sure.

Do you know something you are not telling me?

I shook my head.

Just remember she said, do not talk to any body, do not do any thing stupid and stay away from trouble. Then we will be ok.

I nodded but I did not feel better.

I looked at the floor board but was sleepy so I brushed my teeth and went to bed.

I do not know what I would do if I did not have you Mr Keon. I need you now and can not wait for father to come back and give you the letters. So today I got all the letters from the basement and put them in a envelope and carefully printed your name on it and mailed them. I will keep writing until you write me back. Please write soon or come to 54 Henry street. Wait for mother to be at mah jong first.

Your friend,
Johnny Wong

Dear Mr Keon

Did you ever lie to your mother Mr Keon? Did you lie a lot? My stomach feels funny and I think it is because I am a lier. Not like Mr Ingles but worse because it is to my mother. Yesterday after breakfast I waited around for mother to leave for work but she said she was working a late shift then she said what are you waiting for? Go to school. So I could not look for Rollie's things and hid the hammer and tool under the bed.

On the way to school I imagined what was inside his box under the floor. I guessed millions of dollars or diamonds or guns or disguises or all of it. I thought what would happen if I leave them on Catwoman's door or at a restaurant instead. Then at least nobody could say they were in our house. Then I remembered that mother's finger prints are all over them. So I thought about cleaning everything when mother is out. Then I thought what if its true mother loses at mah jong. Maybe she needs some of this money. Maybe I can sneak some of it before giving it to Catwoman. Then I thought what if Rollie does get caught and really does blame mother. It is all lies but the police might still be suspicious of her and bust her. And maybe Rollie will wear a John Lenin mask and find me and kill me. I wish you could help me now Mr Keon.

How long does the mail take? Maybe I should have just went to Maple Leaf Gardens myself.

Mrs Clover was showing the class pictures of her twins birthday party. Their dad gave them a big wheel that was red like a fire truck and a easy bake oven and a party with lots friends and cake and some clowns. Everybody looked so happy and everything looked so perfect. I did not want to see their perfect family any more so I asked to go to the washroom and just walked around the school.

I saw Barry Arble pulling the overhead projector out of his class so I kept walking. Then I saw the red fire alarm that says pull in case of fire and wondered if it would be hard to pull in case of a for real fire so I tried and it was really easy but then the alarm bells rang and everybody lined up to leave the school. I followed Mr Turner's grade 6 class outside and we all watched the fire trucks come. Even a police car came by. It was a long time before the alarms turned off.

Principal Ingles was really mad and yelled at people to keep quiet. When the fire man left we were allowed back into the school but the principal made everybody who was not in class when the alarm went off line up in his office.

Who pulled the fire alarm he asked. Everybody said not me. Mr Ingles looked at all of us. There was Skinny fart who is the smartest one in Mr Turner's class so I knew she would not be blamed. Lem Keung who was fresh off the boat from Hong Kong and too scared to do anything except math. Wai Woo who was a goody goody two shoes which made me sick and some grade 2s and me. I knew he was guessing who was guilty and he was going to pick me. Then Mrs Suckolove came in with Barry Arble and said to him that Barry was also out of class when the alarm happened.

The principal said Barry's name like he just found the golden ticket. I might have known he said. I will be calling your home again. Everybody else go straight back to class.

Barry looked at me like he knew the truth. But he said nothing. He took the hit for me. Why would he do that Mr Keon?

Your friend,
Johnny Wong

Dear Mr Keon

Yesterday after school mother was home before me. She had cleaned up the room. Instead of watching As the World Turns she sat on the bed with a cigarette. She made me sit beside her. That made me nervous. She reached under the bed and pulled out the paper bag with Rollie's tools.

I saw what's inside Johnny. What are you doing with this?

I did not move. I did not know what to say. I could not breath and my insides hurt like somebody dropped kicked my stomach then reached into my lungs and pulled my stomach out.

What's going on mother asked then took a deep suck from her cigarette.

I kept waiting for her to yell and scream but she did not so I got even more nervous.

You know what these are for Johnny?

I whispered, tools. Hammer and screw driver.

Yes. Tell me what you are doing with them. Tell me.

She almost yelled the last 2 words and scared me. But it was like it almost scared her too because she took a deep breath and just shook her head like she did something wrong.

Does this has any thing to do with Rollie she asked.

No. I found them.

Hammer and screw driver yes. But these are also tools to do bad things. Where you get them?

I wondered how mother knew they were tools to do bad things. I answered, in the lane way.

Where in the lane way.

Behind Catwoman's house.

Are you sure? Are you lying?

Yes. I mean no I am not lying.

Maybe I go ask Catwoman if she knows anything.

Ok I said.

Johnny if you make any trouble, that gwhy low woman will come back and take you away. Was she at your school yet?

I shaked my head.

She said that woman Barbra was at her work asking questions and meant business. She was looking for a reason to separate us forever and make me go live with strangers. Do you hear me? Mother almost yelled.

I nodded.

If she sees you in trouble or doing something bad she will blame me and take you away. Understand?

I nodded again but I do not think she believed me.

She kept the bag with the tools and took them away.

It was like being in a trap. If I listen to Rollie he will leave us alone. If I don't he will rat us out and mother goes to jail. If I disobey mother I get sent away. I was trapped and could not stop thinking about it. The only thing I could think about was how slow mail was and when you were going to come or write back.

Your friend,
Johnny Wong

Dear Mr Keon

I bet you never got picked on at school. I bet you were popular because you were the best hockey player at school and that everyday was good at school. Not like for me. Today everybody left me alone at school. It was almost like they knew I was in a bad mood and was ready to fight someone. Even Mrs Clover did not pick on me even though I kept looking out the window. I thought I might see Rollie watching me. Or Barbra Twomanski coming. Or mother in the back of a police car. I saw Barry was not at school so I thought he got expelled because of me. Then when I went to the office to bring in Sandy Yip because she cut her leg on the yard I saw Barry sitting in the there with the principal and two old people that I thought were his mother and father. All of a sudden I heard a soft voice. It was Barbra Twomanksi. My head speeded up. I wanted to take off but I also wanted to see her.

Hello Johnny we were going to call for you next. How are you she asked.

I lied and said good.

Great stick around I'll get to you I'm almost done here. She said it like she wanted to talk to me, not like she was ready to take me away. Then I heard her say to Barry's parents, its been a rocky start but we expected this. Then she thanked them for coming and told them they could go.

On his way out Barry came up to me to give me a high five like we were best friends but we are not then whispered do not trust Twomanski.

Why would he say that and why would he fake pretend we were friends and give me a secret message?

Get in Johnny the principal said behind his desk as he unwrapped a big fat cigar.

She wore a dress and sat on a chair. I stared at her legs but only because I saw the principal do it. They were crossed. She did not have a hose on.

Sit down Johnny the principal said. Miss Twomanski would like a word with you.

That's when I found out she was not married.

Its nice to see you again Johnny she said. I need help. Can you help me she asked.

I nodded.

There's the sweetest boy I know. He's handsome and really smart but I am worried about him. Do you know why Johnny?

I shaked my head.

Its because I think he's lonely he needs a friend and he needs people who he can count on to look after him. I want to be one of those people. She stopped and looked sad then started again. My problem is he does not want to tell me the truth about what is going on at home with his mother and him. She said he might be scared but there was nothing to be scared of. She thought he needs help and it made her sad that she couldn't help him. She asked if I knew what she was saying.

Yeah really really sad the principal interrupted.

She looked at him like she wanted to say shut up. He bowed his head then he lighted the big fat cigar and went back to looking at his pile of newspapers. I saw one with pictures of soldiers on the streets and a head line that said FLQ Outlawed—250 Rounded Up Under War Measures Act and a $150,000 reward for getting the kidnappers.

She wanted me to help him. She said she was worried because she thought his mother likes to drink alcohol. A lot.

This time I did not nod because I think she was talking about me and the Johnny with the red coat and long black boots. I also guessed that she did not know any thing and was not ready to take me away. Still I wanted to help her because she looked sad and so pretty. Remember Mr Keon that is a secret. But mother said to say nothing and I did not know what to do. Finally I said maybe he does not know what to say. Maybe he just wants people to leave him alone. Maybe he just wants his father to come home. I bowed my head after I said that and started to fake cry except this time it came easy.

I think she saw that and she reached over like she was going to hug me then the secretary came in all mad and told the principal that Barry Arble just peed his name in the kinder garden sand box.

The little prick the principal said.

I stopped crying and wanted to laugh. I remembered that Barry said to not trust her. I did not know what to do. Finally I asked if I could go.

She gave the principal another mad look. Sure Johnny she said. But we will talk again real soon.

Barry waited for me after school. He said Johnny boy

Johnny boy like we were old friends and then he asked if I checked out her foxy legs. He said the principal sure did and had a boner the whole time.

I guessed a boner is a cigar but did I not want to sound like I did not know for sure so I said yes it was a big fat boner.

Then Barry asked did you listen to what I said you gotta watch what you say to her.

I nodded but looked at him like why should I trust you because you are my number 1 enemy then I remembered he did not rat me out about the fire alarm. I asked how he knew Barbra and he said she was his social worker and his parents in the office were really foster parents because Barbra took him away from his mother after she kept leaving him alone in the house which was okay with him but Barbra said his mother has to stop working at the peeler bar and hanging out with bikers.

I know that bikers is like Jack Nickels in Easy Rider because Mrs Clover says he is a yummy bad boy. I think it was in appropriate for her to say that. I did not know what a peeler bar was but I did not want to sound stupid so I said nothing.

So you do not have a father I asked Barry?

Of course I do stupid. Just not here. Somewhere. But I see my mother on Wednesdays at Barbra's office and on some weekends. That is if she's not too drunk to forget.

This time when he called me stupid I did not get mad. But I did feel bad for him. I asked him why he did not rat me out with the principal.

He said he could use a friend who was a killer. We

both laughed. Then he said when the fuzz dropped me off the other day he figured out I only had my mother too. All of a sudden I felt better like I had a friend besides you. But I do not know if I can believe it. It is like that goon John Ferguson who always tries to make you fight but then invites you to watch Star Trek. Would you trust him Mr Keon? Should I all of a sudden trust Barry Arble?

He did not say what happened to his father. But I did not neither.

Your friend,
Johnny Wong

Dear Mr Keon

I can not stop thinking about three things. First is Rollie
will not believe me that mother found the tools. Even if he
does I do not think he will stop making me get his things.
I have to tell him the truth or else try and get the board off
with something else. Second I could not stop thinking that
Barry is the first person I ever met who was taken away
from his mother. That would be as bad as you being traded
to Detroit. But he is not mad about it but I do not know
if I could also not be mad if it happened to me. I started
to think that maybe I should listen more just in case.

Then I was also thinking about Jean. I wonder if Jean
still goes to school and if people pick on him or are now
nice to him because he does not have a father anymore
and I wonder if because he does not have a father is there
is bigger chance of someone taking him away. I think that
if he is from Montreal he must be a Montreal Canadiens
fan but I will not hate him because of it. Mr Keon you are
from Quebec. If you could tell me where I could write to
him then I will.

Mother will not let me go out after school and she is
home everyday now and does not go out to play mah jong
like she used to. I wondered if it was because she was
watching me or did not have the money to play. Any way
I cannot even deliver these letters to you. At least Rollie

will not come over because he thinks the heat is everywhere and he is right. I did see some body sitting in a car for a long time and we seen more police going up and down the street and they even broke up a big party on the street with some other draft dogers that Rollie used to hang out with.

Your friend,
Johnny Wong

Dear Mr Keon

Barry is nice to me now. He is trying to be my friend but I do not know if he will be like Rollie who pretended to be my friend then double crossed me. It is true that Rollie was kind even if he was a murderer. I wonder if he did not kill Meany Ming would he still give me money for using the dictionary because I have used it 37 more times since so that is $1.85 he owes me.

> *Your friend,*
> *Johnny Wong*

Dear Mr Keon

Today was a PD day which is short for party day for teachers and us because there is no school. Mother was not going to let me out but then Barry came over and faked good manners and called her Mrs Wong and took off his shoes when he came in. It worked so mother gave us 3 dollars to go to the pagoda for a double feature of chinese movies. It is always a love story and then a kung fu movie. The first movie was about a rich woman who falls in love with a man then finds out he is dying from a disease and she has to decide if she will stay and look after him except she will lose her family ~~inhairatense~~ inheritance or leave him and keep the money because he will die any way. Many people cried at the end when the man died just after they got married even Barry hided his tears even though he said the movie sucked. When I seen that I stopped thinking that maybe he could be like Rollie. The second movie was about a man who goes to a restaurant owned by really nice people but the people are scared because they owed money to a gang so the man beats everybody up in the gang then helps the restaurant cook and then lots of people come eat. That one was my favorite movie.

After the movies Barry said he wanted to see my best hiding spot before he had to boogie home because his foster mother was a witch and would make him go without dinner if he was late. So we pretended we were the Rat Patrol trapped behind enemy lines and sneaked around Spadina then Darcy street before cutting through the lane way behind Henry street. It was easy to pretend because I was also on guard against Rollie. I showed him the empty garage beside all the other garages that look like little houses ready to fall down. I showed him my bean bag and a collection of sticks that were in a pile in the garage to make arrows and darts and he helped me find some more.

We talked about the $150,000 reward for capturing the FLQ who kidnapped the British diplomat. We decided on what we would do with the money after we saved him. Barry said after saving the limey he would pick up his mother in a taxi and take her to Swiss Chalet and have both the chicken and the ribs and would then find a place Barbra could never find them. I said I would go to see you at every Leafs game and even the road games and I would take him and mother and we would stay in a hotel with a big bed. Then Barry asked if he could just have the money instead of going to the hockey games. I thought that was kind of cheap but said yes.

He liked the garage and the bean bag so much he swore to never tell any body about it and we agreed to call it the secret club house for boys only. Before we left I saw the paint cans where Rollie wanted me to put his package. It looked like they were moved just a little bit because the dust was different. I saw that on Mannix. I started to get scared again but Barry peed the letters FLQ in the corner and said no matter how much you wiggle and dance the last few drops are always in your pants. That made me laugh and forget about Rollie. Barry is very good at making me feel better.

It was a great day because I hardly thought about Rollie except for that one time. And I did not think about Barbra Twomanski and I did not do any thing bad. When I got home I checked for mail from you but another kind of surprise waited for me. A little girl emptied my match boxes from my secret shoe box and was racing them up and down over my hockey cards all over the floor.

I was about to throw her off when somebody said hello Johnny come and meet your sister. That somebody was, my father.

Your friend,
Johnny Wong

Dear Mr Keon

I was so surprised and happy I did not know what to say so I screamed out woohoo. I wanted to hug him but I stopped because he and mother looked like they were ready to fight or already did. Then mother told me to say hello to your father and your sister. But the way she said it it was like father and that girl were thiefs. I recognized my father but I also did not. He had more wrinkles and was shorter than before. But now I see why mother says I look like him.

I was going to show him all my hockey cards but that girl made them go out of order and she folded my Ron Ellis rookie card and she emptied my Batman utility belt all over the floor. I wanted to drop kick hit her in the gut then I remembered promising you to be good and not fight.

Then he took out a present for me. You will not believe what I got. I got double sticks. I heard other people call them num chucks. Then I forgot I had a sister from no where. She was all over my toys and smiled but I did not think it was funny.

I looked at mother because I asked her many times before for the num chuks. But she always said no. She drinked from her tea cup which means she was drinking Johnny.

She slammed it down and said no. She took them

away and said to father that I get into enough trouble and that was the kind of toy that would get me into more trouble.

Sometimes mother is so mean. Why can she not be like Shirley Jones. She is beautiful and drives a bus and sings and is very kind. I bet your mother was like that too.

Mother and father made me and the girl wait in the hall while they talked. I could not understand why mother never said any thing about her plus I could not remember her neither. She asked me if I liked Josie and the pussycats. I do but I did not want to talk to her and said no. Then she started to tell me everything about the show any way like I was stupid. Then she asked me if I liked Barbies and that she hoped to get a Barbie camper van for christmas and that her favourite colours were purple and pink and that her favourite food was shake and bake.

I never even had shake and bake. I looked at her because I could not believe I had a sister and that she could talk so much. Finally I told her to shut up because I wanted to ease drop on mother and father.

I heard everything mother said because she is louder than everybody when she gets mad. She almost screamed when father said he and the girl took Rollie's old room beside ours and that she would go to Orde St School too. Father calls her Jane. I hate that name and I hate her so I came up with a rime. It goes like this Jane is a pain with stains from mane with no brain who plays with planes and trains in the rain by the lane so she must be insane. I will teach Patty Beeso and Barry to say that.

Before dinner father said the men should go out for a walk. That was the first time I was not called a boy by mother or father and it felt good to be a man with my father. We walked down to Baldwin street past Barry's house and around the block. He asked me about school and my teacher and my friends. I said Mrs Clover was a Trudeau lover and hates me.

Doesn't matter Johnny he said. You must always listen to the teachers and respect them.

Mother said this many times but hearing father say this made it sound more important.

I wanted to know why he was away for so long and why he never told us about Jane but I could not. Instead I asked him to take me to see you versus the Boston Bruins.

Sure Johnny. But maybe not against Boston. When I have time. First I need to find work.

I wanted to tell him about Rollie because maybe father would know what to do. But just as I was going to say something father said he knew about him. I almost stopped walking.

He is a bad man Johnny. I am so glad you are safe. I hope the police catch him and his gang fast.

Gang. Was mother in his gang I asked myself? Am I in his gang now?

Are you listening Johnny father said. Until then I am worried for your safety and Jane's safety. So I need you to look after your sister while I am out looking for work. Never should you or her be alone.

I wanted to ask why I have to because it is mother's job and also I never asked for a sister and besides how did I get a sister if father was away. Then it was like he read part of my mind because he said she is your sister and that

is what brothers have to do. Even if they don't want to.
She will start school tomorrow on Monday. And that is
what happened.

Your friend,
Johnny Wong

Dear Mr Keon

Yesterday was supposed to be my second favourite day of the year after Christmas. Halloween. I had a Batman mask and shirt but it was cold so I had to put a jacket over the shirt. Then I had to take Jane with me. She did not have a costume or a mask so father got a paper bag and cut out eyes nose and a mouth and coloured it with black whiskers and called it a cat. Jane cried and cried and said it was ugly. She is a winer but she was right because it was a dum mask. I just wanted to go so I gave her my Robin mask. Finally we went and father came with us. Even though it was cold there were lots of people out.

Our bags got almost full fast. We got lots of my favourite treats like tootsie rolls, razzles and gobstoppers but no snickers. We also got some apples. I do not know why people give out apples. We went up and down Henry street and along Baldwin street then up Beverley street and when we turned onto College street I saw someone across the street with a John Lenin mask staring at me. I stopped because I thought it was Rollie. But then he waved to someone behind us and called out hey John and started to laugh.

We saw that the man behind us was also wearing a John Lenin mask.

There were two John Lenins now but there could not be two Rollies. Then I saw the 2nd John Lenin weared a jean jacket so he had to be Rollie. I was sure. He made a fist and banged up and down like it was hammer or like he was ready to pound someone. He speeded up and turned the corner at Ross street and was gone.

Father reached for me and Jane. Who was that father asked.

I tried to be funny and said everybody knows John Lenin except that is a foney. I am starting to think that father is a bit like the Amazing Kreskin and can see things because he looked like he did not believe me.

All of a sudden I did not care what was in our full bags.

Your friend,
Johnny Wong

Dear Mr Keon

Did you get my letters? If you come father might be home so maybe it is better for you to meet me after school.

Last night I dreamed that a taxi came to our house. Father and I were playing football. Just as he threw a touch down pass to me 3 FLQ kidnappers with hammers and screw drivers got out and kidnapped him.

Father yelled Johnny only you can save me. All you have to do is catch the ball. That is the only way to save me except I could not catch the ball and father got kidnapped and mother and father are separate again because of me. I woke up sweaty. It was so real like in the news except the FLQ all looked like Rollie and spoke french. Since I seen Rollie at the Woolworths I am sure I saw him at Halloween and I am sure he is watching me and waiting and he will keep doing that until he gets his box and goes away.

At school they put Jane into Mrs Echos grade 3 class where she became a teachers pet very fast because she is smart and raises her hand and has a smile that is cute and ~~foney~~ fake. At the first recess she was very quiet and watched everybody. I told her to stay away from some people but I do not think she listened. Then at lunch recess she got into a fight with Cathy Kwan who is the queen of grade 3. They fought about who should be Simen in

Simen says. Jane became Simen after she told Cathy that her for real parents gave her up for adoption which made her run away and cry even though I think it was a lie. Then at the last recess she beat up Bobby Li in grade 5 and said Bobby kissed Wai Woo. Bobby hates girls so I do not believe that is what happened but everybody else does now. That is how she became queen of the yard in her first day of school.

After school she was supposed to meet me in front of the kinder garden playground but Mrs Clover told me to go to the office to get her.

When I got there Mrs Echos said somethings were missing from her desk. She asked Jane if she knew where they were.

Jane said she thinks Cathy Kwan took them.

Principal Ingles had a cigarette in his hand and yelled out to the secretary to see if she knew wear his matches were.

Mrs Echos looked mad at principal Ingles and told him to call Jane's mother.

The principal said you want me to blame the new kid? What if Cathy is your thief and I call the wrong mother. You consitter that. Next thing you know I got me the whole of China town on my doorstep. Don't sweat these ittybitty things Edith.

Mrs Echos left the office and slammed the door.

That was my first time seeing a teacher lose her temper at another grown up. It was kind of funny but I was also mad at Jane for making me go to the office specially when I did not do any thing wrong.

After I took Jane home father surprised me with a Joe Louis to eat. Barry came over so I was allowed to go out for an hour so we went to eat the Joe Louis in the club house but Jane secretly followed us in.

I yelled at her because if father finds out she went off by herself I would get in trouble.

She asked what are those sticks for? What is in the bottles? Can we paint. I want to try the bean bag. Who lives here? I want to play.

I told her only boys allowed and for sure no sisters. But I had to make her go away except I could not let her go alone so Barry and I walked her home. She always does stuff like that. She never stops talking sometimes she sings and she always is moving. She asks lots of stupid questions and she touches all my things. My Spiderman nap sack with all my lego was missing. Father said to be nice and let her play with my things but she is ear responsable and I hate her more than any thing. I do not know if you have a sister Mr Keon but she can not be as bad as mine because mine is from hell or even worse Detroit.

Your friend,
Johnny Wong

Dear Mr Keon

After school I checked for the mail again. If you cannot write because you are on road trip to California that is okay. Just do your best. You can write on the air plane when you have time then you can mail to me when you get back.

Today father raked leaves while Jane jumped into the piles. I got to be alone because mother was not home yet from work. I thought about Rollie's box and decided to get it before he got me. I got a bread knife from the kitchen downstairs and one of mother's shoes for a hammer. The floor board was very tight and I could not put the knife in between the cracks. I banged on the knife. It kept slipping. Finally it stayed and banging made it go deeper .

Johnny? Mother opened the door. I jumped up and blocked her from seeing the knife that was still in the floor. She asked what I was doing with one of her shoes.

I told her I was practising juggling and reached for the other shoe.

See? I threw both shoes up and could juggle a couple of times before dropping them.

She shook her head. Help me make dinner. No time to play.

I left the knife sticking out of the floor and helped make dinner and prayed she did not go back to the room and see it. After I washed some vegetables and the rice mother let me go back upstairs. The knife was still in the floor. I dug around the edges and got it looser. It was like digging for treasure or finding evidence and was kind of fun. Finally I got the board loose enough and lifted it off. I saw something that was rectangular and lifted it out. It was a box made out of gray metal like I seen people put money in. I was right. Lots of money and diamonds had to be inside. I tried to open it but it was locked. I used the knife to break it open but could not. It was pretty light and I shook it around and one thing moved around and some loose things moved so maybe there was no gun but maybe jewels still. I heard mother calling me for dinner so I rushed to put the board back. I hid the box in the closet behind some building blocks that I don't hardly play with no more and ran downstairs.

Your friend,
Johnny Wong

Dear Mr Keon

Did you day dream at school Mr Keon? I'll bet you dreamed about scoring the winning goal in the Stanley Cup final. Mrs Clover caught me day dreaming but I was not really dreaming. I was thinking about what was inside the box and how I was going to let my parents let me out so I could sneak it to the garage. On the way home from school with Jane behind me I told Barry that father was teaching me how to throw a football and that he is a great cook and he likes to take us on walks through the university. Barry did not say any thing. I thought he was a bit jealous that I got my dad back and he does not but maybe he was just being sad so we did not say any thing else until we passed a newspaper box when Barry asked if I heard the big news. I said no.

He said the cops staked out a apartment in Montreal and busted in and caught one of the FLQ kidnappers. They got one who strangled the hostage and stuffed him in a car. I'll bet they beat the crap out of him. His picture is on the front of all the newspapers plus the 3 who got away.

We looked at the pictures. They were Jean's fathers killers. One had the Castro look like Rollie except he looked like he slept on the College streetcar from the be-ginning to the end. 3 of the kidnappers got away. The other hostage is a limey as Barry calls him was still kidnapped and those kidnappers still want their 23 for 1 trade plus money plus an airplane plus the name of the rat who talked to the police plus their magazine read on the news which I think they already did. I asked Barry if he heard any thing about Jean the son of the dead guy. He said no.

I bet the son is very sad. I wonder if the kidnappers stopped to think about Jean before they killed his father because nobody should not have a father. Barry thinks the 3 bad guys who got away are probably going to try and bust him free or kill him so he does not talk or they might go to California. The California Golden Seals are a really bad hockey team except they beat us bad last night. What happened Mr Keon?

At night I kept thinking about Rollie's box and every time mother was in the kitchen or the bathroom I pulled out the box with the knife and tried to open it but it never worked so I had to put it back in the closet.

Your friend,
Johnny Wong

Dear Mr Keon

After school father caught me checking the mail. He asked what I was looking for. I did not know what to say so I told him the truth, that I was waiting for mail from you. Father laughed. How will he know where to find you? He laughed again.

Then I remembered that I did not put my name or address on the envelope. And I did not put a stamp on it either. I wanted to run to the mail box and jump inside but father made me help him rake leaves before it rained and before he had to go to his new job. I was so mad at myself that I raked really hard and the more I thought about it the harder I raked. Father liked that I did not give up even though it was messy work and I worked really hard. I was still mad but I decided to keep writing and this time I would drop the letters at Maple Leaf Gardens for you.

Barry was going to come over after dinner to watch tv. I was going to tell him about Rollie and have him charm mother into letting us go out so I could put Rollie's box in the garage like he said.

But after raking the leaves I went upstairs and saw Jane had all my building blocks piled up high with Rollie's metal box on the top.

Look Johnny it's a balancing box, see.

As soon as she said it the box came crashing down and all the blocks collapsed with them. She has this cutesy giggle I cannot stand and she used it on me. So I exploded and called her a stupid idiot and pushed her out of the way. She fell down but not hard because she was already on her knees but she yelled like her hair was on fire and screamed that I was hurting her. I told her to shut up. Then I saw that the metal box opened but nothing came out. I saw papers and some American money but had to close it fast because I could hear father coming.

Father rushed upstairs. Jane ran to him and said I pushed her head onto the floor. He asked me if it was true. I said yes but before I could explain father said I was grounded and that I could not go out tonight. He felt her head and said there might be a small bump that wasn't there before but wasn't sure.

He yelled at me. Again? How many more times before you really hurt her?

I was going to argue but he did not notice the metal box so I kept quiet even though I wanted to kill Jane. He took Jane to their room and I had just enough time to slide the box under the bed before mother came up.

Mother and I used to eat in our room. She would let me watch tv and I never missed a program. Now we all have dinner in the kitchen at the table. Mother looked at me after father told her what happened. But she was not mad at me. She took my side and said maybe Jane started it. I thought I could not lose with mother covering my back.

Father said it doesn't matter she's a little girl and he has to behave like a big brother.

They argued in front of us over dinner like we were not there and then there was silence. It is like a war in Canada ready to explode like Jane is the FLQ and she has come to break up the country by taking me hostage except I can not decide if mother or father is Quebec and if they will ever get along.

The one good thing is that I got to close the box and push the box under the bed before any body noticed. The other good thing is that father made mother sleep in Jane's room that night after he went to work. That means I was all alone to open Rollie's box.

I stayed up late because I waited until the house was quiet. Then I pulled the box out from under the bed and put it on top like it was a bomb ready to explode. I turned on the light and opened it. There was Meany Ming's dragon pendant. I took it out and looked at it. No wonder Rollie kept it because it is really cool. That was the only jewel. No gun. No disguises. There was lots of American money. It took me a long time to count so much money. Finally I got $135. There was a passport for the United States of America and two drivers licence. Both licence had Rollie's picture. One of them was the name Roland Brown. The other one was Roland Berry. I could not understand why would Rollie have two drivers licence with different names unless he was a spy but he is not. I think. There were some pictures of a little boy who looked like it was Rollie. He looked very shy and with dark hair. There were also lots of pictures of him with his family. It looked like he had a brother and sister. There was one of his sister in the army except she was a nurse smiling with a soldier who was all band aided up. At the bottom of the box were letters. Some of them were from a girl who said she loved him. Those were gross so I put them back. Other letters were from his family. The top one was from his mother. It said Sandra was seriously wounded when her MASH unit was bombed by friendly fire on September 15. I read it again because I did not understand at first that Sandra was Rollie's younger sister. His mother asked him to come home and be with Sandra. That all was forgiven. It was written September 30. I think Meany Ming was killed around then.

This could be all Rollie had left from his home in Maine. I heard mother get up. She would be going down to the bathroom then she was going to check on me. I carefully put everything back after I folded up the letters and organized the pictures into a neat pile then closed Rollie's box and put it under my pillow.

Your friend,
Johnny Wong

Dear Mr Keon

Yesterday was Sunday and it rained so we mostly stayed in the house watching tv. But today was sunny and I should have been in a good mood but I broke a big promise again. Please do not be mad Mr Keon but I got into another fight. After I dropped Jane home after school father let me go out with Barry to the store except he said to pick something up for Jane and come right home. I said yes. I made Barry walk fast because I wanted to drop off Rollie's box. I told him that Rollie left something behind at the house and I wanted to give it to him.

He asked me what it was and I said old pictures and letters which was most of the truth. He wanted to see it. I said no. He said he saw the boring FBI show last night and it said that if I was working with a murderer it is being a accomplish and maybe conspiracy too. I did not know what that means but I already decided I wanted to do this and forget about it finally so I told Barry I did not care and it was none of his business. He was quiet after that which is funny to see because that is two times he was like that after father came back. I do not think he liked me saying that because first father came back and he is jealous and now I have a secret with a murderer.

We got some bazooka joes and walked fast to the lane way to the club house. I made Barry wait outside to be the look out while I hid the box behind the paint cans. But first I opened the box and put in all my money 53 cents and a bazooka joe in case he got hungry. Then we started to rush home because father would be mad if I was out too long. On the way home I remembered that my finger prints were everywhere and mothers was probably still on the pendant. I got so mad at myself and wanted to go back and wipe everything down.

That was a bad time for Barry to tease me. He said Jane was kind of cute. At first I thought he was joking then he said she looks cuter than me which is strange because he says I look like his butt. It was funny but also a really weird thing to say then he asked if I ever noticed that she looks nothing like me. I looked at him because I was confused then he said her skin was a lot lighter and her nose was a lot smaller too. I did not say any thing because I had to think about it then I thought of Jean and his sister who look a bit like only one of their parents. Then finally I said so what?

Barry smiled like he knew a secret then he shook his head at me like I was stupid. He said don't you see your old man couldn't keep it in the barn?

Keep what in the barn I asked him. He made like he was opening and closing a telescope near his dick. Sorry for the bad word Mr Keon. He started to laugh and said your old man's a bad boy then he started to laugh more. I told him to stop which made him laugh even more and he kept laughing and made a song with the words Johnny's dad's nothing but a bad boy bad boy nothing but a bad boy then he made a telescope again and he would not stop so I punched him in the nose and he fell backwards. I think we were both surprised.

He grabbed his nose and saw blood. You stupid little shit he said. Sorry for the swear word again Mr Keon but that is exactly what he said. Then he jumped up and charged me like a wild animal and threw punches and knocked me down.

I tried to cover my head with my arms but I could still feel his punches on my face. At least this fight was not with a girl. Finally somebody came and said that is enough. That somebody was, the Catwoman.

Your friend,
Johnny Wong

Dear Mr Keon

The Catwoman took me to her house. Her cast was off but she had a cane still. I wanted to ask if I could have her cast to put my arm in it in case I had to block Barry's punches again and to beat him over the head with. But I did not. She made me sit in the kitchen. Four cats watched. I did not see Sidney. I asked wear he was.

Don't know. Maybe he found another home. Maybe he wasn't happy here. Maybe he didn't like sharing. She cleaned my face. You're pretty beat up but you will live.

She let me look in the mirror. My face was puffy and scratched up. Mother and father were going to go ape. I sweared I would kill Barry Arble. First he made fun of my father then he said Jane was cute because she looked nothing like me. I started to come up with a rhyme about Barry Arble but only marble rhymes with it and calling him a marble is not funny or mean enough so I stopped.

I asked the Catwoman if she had any brothers or sisters. She said she had a brother in Nova Scotia.

Do you look like him I asked.

She said he's skinnier and looks lots older because he's a fishermen and smokes a lot but people could tell we were brother and sister.

That made me think of Jane. Maybe she was not my for real sister?

Catwoman said she saw new people in my house. She asked if they were family.

I looked away and said yes. Then I told her my father came home with my sister and that I hate her and that Barry says she does not look like me and that made me mad. I did not say anything about the telescope or Barry calling my dad a bad boy.

She opened up a mountain dew and gave me half before sitting down. She said we don't get to choose who we call family. We don't get to choose what they look like or how they behave. But we get to choose whether we want to get along or be mean and nasty. Mean and nasty don't work for no one. Believe me.

I was about to say that Jane is always in my things and gets me into trouble but somebody knocked on the door. That somebody was, the police and my father.

Your friend,
Johnny Wong

Dear Mr Keon

Somebody saw Barry and me fighting and told the police who were just down the street. But it was the same really tall police woman from Ireland who took me home from Eatons so I was not scared of her except I was nervous about my father because I know he would not like me getting into trouble.

Catwoman let them in. Father got so mad when he saw my face. I did not tell him what Barry said or that I punched him first. He made me tell him wear Barry lives.

The police woman said hi again Johnny. I thought it might be you when I heard the description. It's nice to see you again but you're not looking so good. She made me tell her what happened.

I started to then when it got to the part about my father being a bad boy leaving the barn I stopped and looked at father then stared at my feet.

The woman police officer saw that. Then she asked father and Catwoman if she could have a private moment with me.

After father and Catwoman left the room I told her what Barry said and I told her the truth about me starting it.

Well she said it looks like your friend Barry isn't

completely to blame though he went a bit too far. Thank you for being honest with me Johnny. Maybe I'll pay them a visit. I know his foster parents and they won't be very happy with all this.

She was about to leave when I started to ask if they found Roland Berry but I stopped because I am not sure if I wanted to know. Instead I asked her if Canada was having a civil war and if she has to protect important people and guard mail boxes and government buildings from bombs.

She took a deep breath and said everybody is important even the most angry and nasty people. But sometimes a country is like a family. We don't always get along. Some times neighbors don't either. And sometimes solutions are not easy but we will find them. I don't know if the problems in Quebec are coming here but you will be safe. I promise you. She let me touch her beating stick and badge. Then she smiled again and went to Barry's house.

When father came back in he asked me what Barry said. He said I could tell him any thing and ask him any thing except that is your job Mr Keon. It would be cool if you and father were my private advisors. I started to ask why Jane looks different. But I did not finish the sentence.

What father asked? What about her?

I did not answer father right away and he started to look mad so I stared at my feet again and said why does she follow me everywhere?

He said you are her big brother. Your job is to protect her. Just stay away from Barry, do you hear me?

I nodded.

On one hand it was nice to have father stand up for me. On the other hand Barry was my best friend. What if he gets sent to jewvee? What should I do Mr Keon?

> *Thank you,*
> *Johnny Wong*

Dear Mr Keon

I am sorry I did not write to you for a long time and I am sorry my writing is so messy. I could not write because my shoulder was sprained and two bones in my hand had frackchurs. This is what happened.

Barry was not at school since we got into the fight and the police woman came. I thought I got him expelled and sent to jewvee. I did not want that plus that also means I had no one to go out with except Jane and mother and father would not let me out alone. But that day we got out of school early because all the power went out. Jane was now friends with Cathy Kwan so Cathy's mother took them to her house to play. I went to the club house on the way home to see if I could find Barry but he was not there. I checked for the box. It was gone. That meant Rollie got it and he would finally leave me alone and mother and me would not be arrested as part of his gang and mother and father could stay together and I would not be taken away to jewvee. Then a bad thought came. What if Barry took it. He was so mad and he was missing now. Maybe he took the money and ran away.

I went to his house and walked back and forth outside but did not see any body in his house. So I went home and stopped when I saw Barbra Twomanski enter our house. This made me nervous. I took off my shoes and sneaked inside and heard them in the kitchen and peaked around the corner and saw mother and father together with her.

She said she was pleased to see both parents involved with parenting me and asked father if he was working.

Father said he got another new job. This time in the kitchen at Lichee garden restaurant. I got really excited because I heard that sometimes the Maple Leafs go there to eat. He said he would be on the look out for you and get a auto graf for me. That would be as good as getting your rookie card.

Barbra said yum. They have yummy egg rolls. Then she asked where is the girl's biological mother.

Her biological mother? But mother was right there.

Father shrugged his shoulders and said he did not know because her mother deserted Jane not long after the fire. Jane was 2 years old.

Barbra asked how did the fire start.

Father said the fire department think a lit candle fell after her mother dozed off but she denied it. She is not somebody good at taking responsibility. A neighbour smelled smoke then heard Jane crying and called the fire department.

At that second I learned why mother hardly talks to Jane. At the dinner table it is almost like Jane is invisible to her. My mother is not her for real mother. That means father had another wife? If so that means I do not have to be her brother. But my father is her father. I did not get how that could be.

That is when Jane came out of no where and pushed past me and asked mother what is deserted.

At first nobody said any thing.

Mother told her to ask her father but she said it like a whisper like it was a dirty secret.

Father tried to look mad and said to me and Jane that we were supposed to be in school.

But what is deserted Jane asked again.

Nobody said any thing.

Finally Barbra said deserted is when one mother loves you so much that they surprise you by letting someone share their love for you with someone else, like your mother here.

I could see Jane did not get it.

You are lying she said. You are all lying. And you are not my mother.

She kicked at some of my hot wheels then ran out the door and was out of the house before any body moved.

Father said little girls can be so much trouble. He tried to laugh but could not. He reached for his cigarettes but could not find his matches. Father asked mother for her lighter but she said she lost it. That was when I remembered that principal Ingles also lost his matches and Mrs Echos said she was missing things and I was also missing my toy soldiers. I told this to everybody.

Barbra said sometimes children will take things they do not need because they are angry or scared inside.

I said that adds up to 3 lighters and matches gone missing.

Then I thought of the candle that fell and started a fire when Jane was a little girl and her mother was asleep.

Then we all looked at each other like we were thinking the same thing.

Barbra said she could not have gone far.

Father was the first one out the front door but Jane was no where. He called out to her. Everybody else came out.

Mother said she would go up the street to College and told father to go down to Baldwin street. She asked Barbra to look after me at home. So mother and father went up and down Henry street calling for Jane. Soon other people on the street came out to see what was going on and they joined in the hunt too.

I put on my running shoes and was ready to go when Barbra put a hand on my shoulder and stopped me.

I told her I know all the good hiding places.

She looked up and down the street. We heard people calling Jane who did not answer. Okay Johnny, she said. But first get your coat while I call the police. Wait for me and we will go together.

I got my coat but she took a long time on the phone so I jumped into Rat Patrol speed and ran out the house. I climbed the fence that led to the lane way. When I got there I thought about going straight to McCaul street but there would be lots of people there and not many good places to hide. But if I went right I would be in the long lane way behind Henry street there would be lots of places to hide. Including the secret boys club house. The lane way was empty but I could hear people yelling out Jane. The club house was only a few houses down so I got to it very fast. The door was closed. It would not open. Something was blocking the door. I looked through the cracks. Even though it was still day time it was very dark inside. I could see nothing but I could hear a little sound like a scratch on something hard. Then it happened again. Then I could hear someone breathing. That someone was Jane. I heard the sound again and a small light. Through the crack I could see Jane moved the pile of sticks that were supposed to be the darts and arrows onto the top of the bean bag. She made another sound. That's when I knew it was matches.

Jane I shouted. Jane. Stop let me in.

She looked up at me and stopped lighting matches. Go away. You are not my boss. You are not my brother. Leave me alone.

Then she lighted another match and threw it in the pile. Soon a small flame lighted up the whole garage and I could see her throw a whole pack of matches and a lighter into the fire. This made the fire jump and smoke began to fill up the garage. Jane started to cough.

Jane Jane open the door, I yelled.

She turned to me but dropped to her knees coughing and coughing. I looked around for help but the laneway was empty. I banged on the door.

It would not open. I charged into it with a drop kick and could feel it move. Then I ran at it with my shoulder. My shoulder hurt like someone shot me there and the door opened so fast that I fell on the ground in pain inside the garage. I saw that the small pile exploded again and caught onto the wall. It got very very hot and the smoke choked me and stung my eyes so that I could hardly breathe or see. I found Jane on the ground. She stopped choking and was not moving. Just like that the whole inside was on fire and we were surrounded by flames. I tried to pick Jane up but could not and fell on her. I tried to cover her from the fire. Something fell on my hand and I wanted to scream but could not.

Then somebody grabbed me under my arms which hurt because I could not lift my arm. Then he yelled out keep your feet moving keep your feet moving. That some body was, Barry Arble.

He dragged me backwards outside then ran back inside for Jane. But he did not come back out right away. I tried to yell out to him and Jane but I kept coughing and was almost blind from the smoke. The roof of the garage came crashing down just as I thought I saw someone dragging a body to the door. I saw him fall with his clothes on fire. And that was when I blacked out.

Your friend,
Johnny Wong

Dear Mr Keon

I did not tell you that when I woke up in the hospital father and mother were there. Mother was crying like I never seen before. I asked them what happened because I could only remember Barry dragging me out of the garage but not Jane. This time it was father's turn for his eyes to water up but he did not cry all the way. He said Jane is ok. She got really lucky. Everybody did but maybe not so much Rollie.

Rollie? I asked.

He said Rollie dragged Barry and then Jane out of the fire but he suffered very bad burns. He will never be the same again.

I got tired very fast just listening. After mother and father left I could not fall asleep but then I cried and don't remember any thing else.

I forgot to tell you that Barry and I were in the same hospital after the fire. The first time I went to his room he was sleeping. He snores. He had big bandages wrapped around his arms and body. The next time I went to visit him the nurse just finished feeding him ice cream.

Johnny boy Johnny boy, how's my man? He said quietly but with a smile. He looked very tired and weak.

I smiled and said hi.

He looked at the door then said that nurse was foxy, hey?

We both laughed.

I said I am happy because the Leafs won last night and you scored and was named first star.

Doesn't matter he laughed Esposito and Orr will destroy them in the playoffs. If they even make it.

Shuuut up I said.

We talked a bit about what was on tv and how stupid principal Ingles was and then we got quiet.

Finally I said I was sorry for hitting him.

He said, that's ok, you got a slick right jab, I didn't see it coming.

Yeah, well it was kind of cheap.

I guess I kind of lost it too.

Your parents came by again, he said.

I nodded.

They keep bringing these shrimp and whatever these balls are. It is like I'm a god to them. They also brought me a GI Joe and these comics.

I looked at the haw gow and shoe mie. Mother would have made them fresh. Barry did not touch them and I knew he would not. I said well you did save me.

That's right I'm a hero. He smiled and tried to laugh but coughed instead.

I thought you ran away or something because you were gone for days after our fight.

He said his foster witch grounded him after the cop came and she made him miss his next visit to his mother. So he took off any way. Twomanski and the police brought him back the next day. Then the foster witch got really serious about the grounding and he was stuck at home.

So what were you doing at the garage, I asked.

He said I heard half the neighbourhood calling out for your sister. I figured she ran away too. And our club house is the best hiding spot. I took off and when I got to the laneway I saw you charge into the garage. I could hardly see you through the smoke.

I do not know why it is easier to say sorry than thank you but I could not thank him for saving me. Maybe it is easier for me to write than it is to say things. So I told him he snores.

Your friend,
Johnny Wong

Dear Mr Keon

Sometimes my shoulder and hand still hurts. I had to stay in the hospital for sick kids for three days and I had to go back to change the bandages. I also had a cast. It was much smaller than Catwoman's was so I could not get many things signed on it. After I got out of the hospital I had to go to a foster home. I thought that was unfair because father just came back. Barbra said Jane and I almost died under our mother and father's care. Until mother and father could prove they could work together and keep us safe and mother stops drinking I would have to stay with the foster family. My sister Jane was already there. I was really scared about it for so long but it is not so bad. I finally got to eat beefarowknee and the foster mother has dessert everyday. Jane and I have our own rooms. I showed it to Catwoman. I have two posters of you and one of the Fantastic Four and of the Mod Squad but that one was from who ever lived here before. Barbra let Catwoman visit me at my foster parents. She was going to sign my cast Johnny On the Spot because she says it means one who responds to an emergency and somebody you can count on. I said that was nice but it also means a porta potty. She said you are right and we both laughed. She dared me to let her sign and I did and she signed it with beautiful printing.

She told me Sidney the cat finally returned. It looked like he got into some scraps because fur was missing and there were scratches. Catwoman thinks he probably got into another animal's territory. Animals may wander but they need to belong somewhere she said. She also said that even cats need a home of their own. Certainly people do and we'll do crazy things to find it.

I guess that means everybody. Rollie the FLQ Barry me Jane. I always listen to make sure my sister is ok and I always make sure I know where she is at home and school and everywhere else. I look for matches and lighters even though nobody in the house smokes. Just in case. Jane has to go talk to someone about why she hid her sadness and to let her feelings out better. I let her guard all my toys and hockey cards.

Your friend,
Johnny Wong

Dear Mr Keon

I was so happy to see that you scored against Los Angeles. I think you could win the sportsman award again this year. I did not tell you but I do not have to hide these letters like before. Gladys my foster mother gave me a notebook. She said she would personally mail them to you at Maple Leaf Gardens. She promised to remember to put my name and address and a stamp on the envelope. I still hope you will write back or visit me even if it is at Gladys house.

Barry was in the hospital a long time and had to go back a few times to change his bandages. One time he had to stay because the pain was so bad. But tomorrow they will take the last of his bandages off and he will go back to his foster parents. Too bad he does not get to go home to his mother and too bad we were not in the same foster home. He said he has burn marks that will never go away but he did not show them to me but that is good because that would have been gross because I have some skin that is going to be different colour now too. Gladys let me go see him and he would save me all his leftover food even melted ice cream. My mother and father also still visited him in the hospital and in the foster home on Baldwin Street. Mother still makes him dumplings. She said she will always have a plate ready for him like he was family.

I guess that makes us like brothers. Maybe he will find his for real father too.

We said we would write to each other but I know he hates to write. He should try. It is not so hard.

Thursdays is the day mother and father have to go to talk to someone and show that they are ready to be parents, especially mother. Mother always did her best to protect me and besides I do not understand why we could not just stay with father. But maybe soon Jane and I can go home and if Barry is still on Baldwin St we will be neighbours at least.

Your friend,
Johnny Wong

Dear Mr Keon

Today on the same day Barry got his bandages off the last hostage James Cross got out after 62 days. The FLQ kidnappers finally let him go. But they did not get their money or their 23 for 1 deal. They also did not get the rat. Maybe they were like teenagers like Rollie said and were asking too much. But they still got a good deal because they got to go on a air force plane to Cuba. The 3 FLQ guys who killed Jean's father and got away are still on the run.

> *Your friend,*
> *Johnny Wong*

Merry Christmas Mr Keon.

Sorry I did not write in a long time. My hand still hurts even though it is supposed to be healed. The doctor calls it cronic pain and that there might be some nerve damage. But today mother and father gave me 2 packs of hockey cards and a Mattel Secret Agent Set. It is a gun that has a camera a radio and a ruler. Jane did not get the Barbie camper van she wanted. But she did get some new crayons and a doctor and nurse kit.

> *Your friend,*
> *Johnny Wong*

Dear Mr Keon

The newspapers said they finally got the last 3 FLQ guys who killed Jean's father. They got trapped in a tunnel. I wonder if they had a shoot out. I also wonder if Jean wants them dead or in prison forever or if he just wants to forget about it. But I do not think any body can forget about losing their father. I wish I knew what happened to Jean. My family might get back together but his never can. It will never be the same again for him. At least he has a sister. I want to tell him that she is still his sister even if she looks different. Mr Keon if you can get me his address I will write to him too brother to brother.

The newspapers also said Rollie's charges have been changed from lots of break ins and 2nd degree murder to just the break ins and in voluntary man slaughter. Gladys said that is a good sign for Rollie and that him killing Meany Ming was not something he tried to do on purpose. Plus he saved two children after that and it cost him 3rd degree burns. I wanted to visit him but Gladys said no. But today I got a letter from him.

Dear Johnny

Somebody else is writing this letter because the nerves in my hand have been destroyed and I cannot grip a pen. The funny thing is that I feel nothing. A while back I told you about a book I was reading. The main character was Holden. He was angry and very unhappy and never felt like he belonged. I said America was like that before and now Canada was too. Just look at the FLQ. It turns out I was a lot like that too. I was lost, angry at my country and just confused about things and people. I was also naive. That usually leads to dumb decisions and hurting people.

I was ready to hop the border and take my chances and head home. Then a Bazooka Joe and 53 cents taught me something that Holden never learned. That a new home and a new life and feeling like you can belong can happen anywhere. You and your mother were my best friends. I am sorry for all the pain I caused. I never wanted anything bad to happen to anybody. I just wanted to start a new life but never had my head on straight to do it. Then something bad happened in my family and I just lost it. I am glad you have your father back and you finally get to go to a Leaf game.

I was on my way back to the garage to leave something for you—Dave Keon's rookie card. Unfortunately, it got burnt in the fire. I hope you can get another one someday.

Your friend,
Rollie

P.S. GO LEAFS GO

Dear Mr Keon

I hope you will not be jealous but I wrote a letter to Rollie. He is a murderer but also a rescuer. I wrote in my best printing and double checked the spelling and punctuation. It goes like this.

Dear Rollie

Thank you for writing to me. I have written many letters but father and you are the only people to ever write a letter to me. I was going to write back sooner but mother said it was a bad idea and that I would get into trouble. Finally Barbra said it was ok because you saved Jane and Barry's lives when you did not have to and you almost died. Jane and I are home right now for a long Christmas visit. We had to go to a foster home after the fire. Still I wish they would have let us stay with father. Sometimes I hate Barbra for that. But I do not want her to die. She will not say when we get to go home for good. I hope it will be soon. I know you will not get to go home to the United States for a long time. But maybe when I am old enough I can visit you. Until then I will write to you, man to man.

From your friend,
Johnny Wong

p.s. Please do not be jealous but Dave Keon is now my friend too.

Author's Note

Biographical aspects: Though fictionalized, I wanted to bring many personal and historical elements together. I was born and raised in downtown Toronto as the son of Chinese immigrants. Though a boy at the time, I have vivid memories of this era—the draft dodgers partying on Baldwin St, my hippie teacher, and the FLQ. I lived on Henry St., and went to Orde St. Public School. Many of the names and personalities of the characters are derivatives of actual people. My father really worked as a chef at Lichee Garden. However my mother couldn't stand alcohol. I was of course a hockey fanatic who worshipped Dave Keon, and I did mail the Toronto Maple Leafs, forgetting both a stamp and a return address.

Acknowledgements

Greatest thanks to the Usual Suspects ...

Trish Lucy, my smarter half, who not only does everything for me except cook, she makes everything possible and better.

My critiquing and writing wizards of many years who tell it like it is and how it should be, re-shaping and re-moulding lumps of words into something discernible: Chris Crowder, Amy Tector and Alette J. Willis.

My brilliant beta readers: Doreen Arnoni, Marc Brown and Mary Gellner, and of course my sharp editor Julie Roorda.

My talented nephew Avery Ng who illustrated a kick-ass cover at age fourteen, and Erica Russell for her artistic advice and expertise.

Michael Mirolla and Guernica Editions for merging old school decency with a thirst for borderless originality.

About the Author

Wayne Ng was born in downtown Toronto to Chinese immigrants who fed him a steady diet of bitter melons and kung fu movies. Ng works as a school social worker in Ottawa but lives to write, travel, eat and play, preferably all at the same time. He is an award-winning short story and travel writer who continues to push his boundaries from the Arctic to the Antarctic, blogging and photographing along the way at WayneNgWrites.com. Wayne's first novel, *Finding the Way: A Novel of Lao Tzu*, was released in 2018 (Earnshaw Books). He has also completed his third novel, a contemporary family drama.